Only At Ainsworth

A Novella

Heather M Lewis

Edited by: Larissa Lewis
Cover Design by: Katarina

Dad,

High five, low five, baby five

Other works by Heather M Lewis

Recalling Theodora
Wherever They Go

1

Greetings from Ainsworth

Hansel Park's office was anything but welcoming. For starters, the bulbous writing desk that he frequently sat behind took up a majority of the room. Then, there were the dilapidated bookcases whose warped shelves threatened to break at any minute. Worse than the furniture was the airflow, or better yet, the lack thereof. The windows were nailed shut shortly after Hansel moved in. His habit of smoking cigars didn't help.

Despite the health risk it posed to his lungs, he

claimed that smoking helped clear his mind. And maybe it did. His guest could never agree or disagree, as they were too preoccupied with holding their breath so that they didn't choke on the stale air that surrounded them.

Located within a Victorian-era building, Hansel's literacy agency, Ainsworth Press, occupied a room on the third story. In the twenty-five years he'd owned and operated Ainsworth Press, he'd signed eighteen writers. Each writer who ventured into the office brought their own charm and creativity that captivated Hansel. Some wrote romances, while others concentrated on futuristic fantasy. No matter what the authors wrote, Hansel read with intense interest. The novels brought life—a break from the mundane. And he hoped that the writer sitting in front of him, Finley Glover, would accept his offer and become the nineteenth author he signed.

"As I was saying, we here at Ainsworth Press are beyond thrilled that you considered us," Hansel said. "I've read over your manuscript five times! Each time, I'm blown away by the vivid descriptions, the engaging dialogue, and the originality. You must tell me what inspired you to write a cowboy adventure novel? It's completely against the current popular trend in fiction. Nowadays, everyone is caught up in the whole Red Scare. Spies here, spies there, spies everywhere. But not you. You went with cowboys and lost gold. Tell me why?"

After speaking his lengthy plea, Hansel pressed his fingertips together and leaned forward, indicating that he was ready for a great explanation.

Finley was grateful for the chance to talk. Up until that point, he was focusing on the environment he found himself in. Mostly, his mind was filled with questions, like how Mr. Park wasn't bothered to work in such a sullied office. Finley was far from being the neatest person, but the stains, smears, and suspected mold were startling. *Were the cleaners on strike due to low pay?* Finley wanted to joke. Yet, he didn't. There was no need to put the wrong foot forward.

Fortunately, for Finley, the stench of smoke and faint scent of urine didn't upset his stomach or nose. In fact, the smells went right over his head. He'd built up tolerance during the war. No smells could be worse than those he'd experienced in the field. *Had Mr. Park gone off to war, too*, Finley wondered. He was about the right age.

"Well, it's like you said, communism has taken everybody's imagination and run rampant," Finley began. "To be completely honest, I've read several of those types of books, and if I'm being frank, they're all the same—there's hardly any difference between them! Sometimes, the protagonist is a former pilot, bomber, playboy; other times, he's a battle-hardened soldier plagued with rough memories."

Finley paused for a short breath. As he did, Hansel stopped nodding. His penetrating gaze, however, remained on Finley.

"But cowboys—why that topic? I don't think before your novel, I've ever read a fictional account of cowboys."

"I've long since held a special interest in cowboys. It started when I was rather young," Finley explained with a chuckle. "It was my father who first told me about cowboys. I was a lad sick with the flu. It was the only time I ever saw my dad frightened." As the words flowed from his mouth, he took his eyes off Hansel's and glanced out the window, which could do with a bit of cleaning. "As I tried to fall asleep with a high fever, my dad regaled me with tales from the Wild West. He'd said that while he read the tales in dime store novels, they were based on real events. That was how I came to learn about Billy the Kid, Doc Holliday, and Calamity Jane. Even though I was in a rough spot, and it took me quite a while to get well, whenever I think about the Wild West, I think of my dad, and suddenly, I'm calm."

"Through your writing, you are trying to give your readers the same feelings of comfort and nostalgia," Hansel theorized.

"I suppose so. With whatever I write, I hope to take the reader out of their current environment and launch them into a place they've never been."

"Escapism," Hansel said with a firm nod. "It's more important than people can ever imagine. Nothing pleases me more than ending my day with a good book. My passion for books started when I first learned how to read. It hasn't simmered down in the least. I suppose it's my love of books and fine storytelling that propelled me to start my own literary agency."

"You've been quite successful," Finley said enthusiastically. "Some of the authors you've helped to publish are some of my favorites. There's Simon Bixby and Dylan Newham. I could read a Newham book until the binding splits open. Even so, I daresay, I'd still read the book."

Looking modest, Hansel bowed his head. "While at times I give in to my ego and think I have done great wonders for the literary world, I also have to step back and give acknowledgment to those authors who have trusted me to share their stories with the world, as I'm hoping you will be doing."

Finley spread his hands apart. "I'm interested in the prospects Ainsworth Press might offer. At the end of the day, I want nothing more than for my book to be in the hands of readers. Yet, I'd hate to misstep and make a rash decision that could derail that from happening."

"I completely understand. Completely! You

see, most authors have reservations about trusting just any agency. Those who don't write might think that authors would gladly sell their souls, as it were, to have their books in print and distribution. That, however, is far from the truth. The truth of the matter is that authors want to make sure that not only are they getting the best deal, but also their book. More than one author that I've signed expressed interest in their book having a long legacy."

Finley murmured his approval at the other author's viewpoint.

Hansel carried on, "Now with that being said, perhaps it's best to expand on Ainsworth and what it has to offer. We are far from being the grandest literary agency, but we do have steady sales. We work extremely hard on behalf of our authors. Our strategies and marketing teams have done wonders. The proof is in the pudding, so to speak. For starters, we have not one or two bestsellers—but seven! For such a modest company, that is quite an accomplishment. Let's start with the negatives and then work our way to the positives."

Folding his hands together, Finley recrossed his legs and settled into the faded red cushioned chair that had seen better days. Ainsworth Press hadn't been the first literary agency he'd reached out to. In fact, it'd been his fifth. The first three flat-out rejected him. The response letter stated his book was not "current" or "marketable." Their thanks for reaching out and good wishes in getting his book published somewhere else provided little comfort. The fourth, which he'd reached out to a month ago, had yet to send a reply. He reckoned no news was good news.

As Hansel was saying, the royalties would be on the smaller side. Since Ainsworth relied heavily on contracting out work for illustrators and editors, they'd have to pay more for those services. The money would have to come from some of the revenue from Finley's sales. The only other negative was that the press tour, if there was one, would have to be relatively small. If he had a wide circle of friends, could they be trusted to help spread the word about the book's publication?

"That's enough of the bad," Hansel said with a deep laugh. "Now let's move on to the good."

Finley loosened the pressure of the grip holding his hands together. Internally, he prayed that the good would outweigh the bad, as the bad was pretty horrible. No marketing team? What was he supposed to do? Pitch up a table at busy intersections, asking pedestrians and commuters to buy his book? That defeated the entire purpose of going with a literary agency.

Royalties, Hansel was saying, they matter. Didn't they? Finley found himself involuntarily nodding. Yes, he wanted royalties. While his daughter, Eve, had yet to outright say that she wanted to attend university to study art, Finley was a hands-on dad who knew well enough of his daughter's hopes and desires. Besides, he'd seen her sculptures, and if he knew anything, he knew that others should see them too. They'd do their best with five percent. With all the strength he could manage, Finley successfully managed not to react negatively.

But how could he support her education with little to no royalties? What he was hearing was horrible. All of this was absolutely rubbish! Why had Hansel invited Finley to London just to have a chat with him in such a small, dismal, cramped space? Couldn't he have just responded to Hansel's written inquiry?

"Do we have a deal?" Hansel's voice was flat, completely void of emotion.

Did they have a deal? No. They did not have a deal. But did Finley have the fortitude to say as much? No. He did not.

"Truth be told, I'm a slow processor. I'm afraid I need more time to think over the terms you've presented."

"Of course," Hansel replied. From his right breast pocket, he retrieved a fat cigar.

Was Finley's imagination playing games with him, or did the look in Hansel's eyes seem both pleased and surprised that Finley hadn't flat-out rejected him? Should he have just said no?

"Thank you again for taking the time to meet with me." Finley extended his right hand, and the two men shook. "I'm afraid I must cut this short, as I have an appointment later this afternoon. I do appreciate you for having considered me worthy of being represented by your agency. At your earliest convenience, you will mail over the terms you've just listed?"

"Of course, but are you sure you must leave so soon? I was hoping to discuss your book in greater detail. As I've said before, it truly is one of a kind. Surely, I can pick your brain to get a better understanding of how you formed such a work?"

Finley couldn't say for sure, but in that moment, he sensed desperation. But why? Hansel must surely be a busy man. He owned a literary agency after all. Why was he insisting on further discussions about a book that Finley had not yet agreed to publish?

"How about this?" Finley said casually, suppressing his growing irritation at being stuck in the office. "You seem to be quite the reader. What criteria does a book need to have to catch your interest? You've mentioned my book is unique. Is that all you're looking for in a book?"

"Yes, I am an avid reader. A bookworm, if you will," Hansel stuttered as he tucked the cigar back in his pocket. It was clear he hadn't been expecting Finley to answer his question with a question. "As

I've said before, reading can serve as a form of escapism. I think all well-written books, no matter their genre, deserve an opportunity to be read and appreciated."

"But originality—is that your one criterion for agreeing to sign an author? Does the author themselves not matter? Would you be willing to sign a problematic author?"

Hansel leaned forward and rested his forearms on the writing desk. His left cuff link landed in a small brown liquid droplet. "Yes and no. You see, not every idea has to be original if it's uniquely told. Humankind has been writing books for centuries. Every idea has been told that will ever be told. Sure, people will squabble back and forth about who wrote what first, but does it truly matter? At the end of the day, it's the creativity employed by the author that will determine if the book is a success. The most advertised book can be forgotten about. The impression left by a book on the reader will not be forgotten. As far as the authors, well." Hansel paused and thought carefully about proceeding, "How well can another person really know another? There can always be skeletons in one's closet. While I do support the author, my focus is on the book. I'm sure my authors appreciate the fact."

Without missing a beat, Finley changed topics. "Your passion for books is impressive and sincere.

Have you ever considered being an author your-self?"

"Me?" Hansel said as he placed his right hand on his chest and gave an incredulous laugh. "No. I don't think writing is my strength. I've made attempts, but the results were not to my liking."

"I might not go down in history as one of the best authors, but I can tell you this, and please trust me when I tell you this, as I take this to heart: a person only becomes a good writer by writing. Repetition is key. Thinking about writing is not enough. Reading is a good way to improve one's writing, but that alone will not help the writer develop their skills. In the beginning, assuming you haven't written before or very much, you will write terrible sentences. You will write sentences that will make you want to burn the paper before you. But you don't burn the paper. No, you leave the matches on the mantle. Instead, you reach for a new sheet of paper, and you start again. You must always start again. I do. Many others have. Don't feel embarrassed by how many takes are needed to create the perfect sentence to form the greatest paragraph. No, be proud of the effort you're making! I've been to several author conferences. You'd be surprised at how many authors delayed their career because they didn't think they had the skills needed to write."

Finley paused before delving into the subject of inspiration. Writing works of fiction that one feels passionate about comes from inspiration, which can be found anywhere. Sometimes in the mundane aspects of life or moments of sadness. But also, during times of happiness and relaxation, like listening to one's favorite song and wondering what motivated the composer to create the tune.

Lastly, he touched on how writing can connect to new starts in one's own life. Whenever he thought back to a novel he'd written, he could trace it back to a significant milestone in his life. Eve had just taken her first steps when he'd started his eighth novel. Her walking inspired him to refocus the novel: it became about a lone cowboy who'd been stranded in the middle of the Mojave Desert. Alone with his Colt revolver and trusted Quarter Horse, he'd have to survive by any means possible.

Unlike earlier, he didn't feel as self-conscious when he spoke. Deep down, Finley knew it was probably the last time he'd ever speak to Hansel since he had no intention of accepting the offer presented to him by Hansel. So, if he says something foolish, he wouldn't deal with any repercussions. Besides, if Hansel insisted on keeping Finley trapped in the miserable office, the very least he could do was listen to Finley discuss a topic he appreciated.

Hansel didn't nod. He blinked rapidly. "I think I get what you're saying, and I completely agree. Yes, new starts—new stories need to be told." He spoke slowly, almost reluctantly.

"If you've got the time to read other people's stories, you've got the time to tell your own. That's how I think about it."

"Tell your own story," Hansel mused, stroking his chin.

"I really must be on my way. I do have a train to catch. Thank you again for taking the time to meet with me. I hope my tirade didn't frighten you. If you ever find yourself in my neck of the woods, don't be afraid to pop in for a quick chat."

Hansel once again accepted Finley's hand and watched him depart from his office with his hat in his hand and brown over coat draped over his left arm. *Tell his story*, he thought, as the office door closed shut. Did he have the time to write a story? No. It didn't hold any interest. But a new start. A chance for his story to be told through whichever medium possible enticed Hansel.

Just the thought of people knowing about him and what he'd done in his lifetime caused a surge of energy and excitement to ravage his body. Hansel leaped up from the chair he was sitting in. For twenty-seven years, he'd occupied the space. And he hated it—all of it. He despised the walls. They started off as a dainty pale yellow but had become almost completely gray on account of the dirt and smoke. Dust coated most of the furniture, while stains from tea and coffee that he couldn't be bothered to clean dotted the carpet and accent rugs. He couldn't care less if tomorrow all of it was gone. In fact, it should be gone. All of it.

In a bizarre, almost manic fashion, Hansel started to erratically pace the floors. He wasn't lying when he said he lacked the ability to write. He'd tried. To his critical eye, he didn't possess the creativity and flair that the others he'd signed had. But what if he inspired another to write his story? Journalism could be the medium to present his life story.

Pausing in front of the door that led to the bedroom, Hansel cocked his head slightly to the right. His eyes held a focused look as if he were trying to see through the off-white-colored door that desperately needed a thorough wipe down. Wait, what day was it? Tuesday. Yes, a Tuesday was as good as any other to start anew.

The sound of his front door creaking open snapped him from his thoughts. "Mornin', old boy. Do you have time for a quick word? I need your advice on what tie to wear for an interview I have today."

Hansel smiled sweetly, "Come on in, Bart."

2

<u>More Tea, Please</u>

If there was one thing Martha did well, it was to hate passionately. Once she disliked something, it was hard for her not to dislike it. She was so stubborn that more than one member of her immediate family called her Bullie as a childhood nickname. Not that she was mean to others. In fact, in a brash and coarse way, she was actually very nice to others. No, she was called Bullie because she was as stubborn as a bull.

One thing she hated, and had hated for a good

bit of time—her entire life to be exact—was her name. Why on Earth had her parents given her such a colonial name? Was she supposed to milk the cows and mend the fences in her free time? All of her sisters were given prettier names like Grace and Clare. Not her, though. She was shackled with Martha. It was the most preposterous name. When she was ten, she tried going by her middle name, Jane, but her parents weren't having it. Her name was Martha, so she would be called Martha, even if she didn't like it.

Rivaling the hatred of her name was the hatred she had for rude customers. Her tea shop, Tea Time, was a small hole-in-the-wall operation. If a person didn't see the cute, whimsical sign above the doorway, they'd miss the shop entirely. The shop was so small that many of her customers were repeat customers who'd first visited the shop when it opened over a decade ago.

It was a simple operation, really. Offering a variety of tea at a fair price, Tea Time was meant to serve those who'd either missed their morning tea or needed a quick pick-me-up. Opening at six in the morning and closing at two in the afternoon, the shop had done remarkably well. The surplus in revenue caused Martha to think that she might be able to open another Tea Time.

The business was not without its own set of challenges, though, one being difficult customers.

As owner and general manager, it was her responsibility to put rude customers in their place. She was rather skilled at the activity, yet whenever she found that her own staff was the cause of the disturbance, she often became flushed with emotion. It wasn't uncommon for her ears and cheeks to turn red. When Natalie McDonald, her newest hire, came back and told her of the situation unfolding, she prayed that it wasn't Natalie's fault. That morning, she had more than enough on her plate.

"Good morning, sir. What seems to be the issue?" Martha said pleasantly to the man who wore an irritated expression on his face.

"Why don't you tell me?" he said, thrusting his paper cup in Martha's face.

Thinking he was intending to throw the contents on her face, she flinched and backed away. He muttered an apology and lowered the cup. He asked her again to look inside.

Cautiously, she looked down and inspected the contents of the cup. The tea's coloring indicated that a generous portion of milk had been poured. The color of the tea was not disturbing. The white clumps were. Something was wrong with the milk.

"What milk canister did you use?" She asked quietly so that no nearby customers overheard her.

"That one in the middle," he jabbed his right index finger at the tall steel canister positioned on a countertop three feet away.

"Oi, Brandon," she called out. "Give me a fresh black, will you?"

Brandon Whitely, a university student, obliged and filled a red paper cup with freshly brewed black breakfast tea. It was a shame that she had to experiment with the most popular types of tea, but the aroma from the tea in the angry customer's cup indicated a breakfast tea, and she needed to get to the bottom of the situation.

With the cup of steaming hot tea, she and the customer navigated through the clueless customers. Skipping any unnecessary dramatics, she pushed back the sprocket of the canister and carefully observed a steady stream of cold white milk from the stout. After a considerable amount landed in her cup, she removed her hand from the sprocket and glanced down. And then waited. No white clumps appeared. She didn't have time to react as the customer reacted first.

"That young man over there, the one cleaning off that table. He must have switched the canisters."

The young man in question was Eric Carmen, who'd spent most of the morning cleaning the back of the shop. The smell of bleach still hung in the air from when he cleaned the floors. To the best of her knowledge, Eric only left the back to assist Natalie when she was having difficulty with the cash register. Martha knew very well that no canisters were switched. They never switched canisters. Hardly ever had they run out of creamer or milk.

Feeling triumphant, Martha felt confident and secure enough to say in a soothing voice, "How about we get you a new cup of tea?"

"Nonsense," the man sputtered, his face red with embarrassment.

"If you don't want a new cuppa, how about a refund? That's all I can do."

"That's all you can do? Hardly! I demand a voucher. You tried to deceive me. Imagine if I had drunk this? I might have ended up in the hospital."

With considerable effort, Martha held her tongue and did not pull a face. Upon hearing his outrageous request, her initial response had been to ask if he didn't trust her milk the first time, why would he trust her a second time? Not wanting to cause a scene or make the customer more emotional, she responded firmly but kindly.

"Tea Time does not provide vouchers. This is a small establishment. If you don't want a refill or a refund, I'm afraid there's nothing I can do for you."

"Establishment," he said with a smirk. "That's a bit far-fetched, isn't it? I will report you for this."

"I'm terribly sorry that you're unsatisfied with my offer." Pressing her hands together as if in prayer, she added softly, as if talking to a child throwing a temper tantrum, "If there's nothing more I can do for you, perhaps you could leave the store. I must consider the other customers, you see."

"How dare you throw me out! Do I look like rubbish?" With that, he raised his right arm, turned, and launched the paper cup. The now-warm tea landed on the pale green wall that held the mural of various-sized decorative teacups.

Martha had gone out on a limb to have the mural completed. In the beginning, she thought it would give the shop originality. But when the first few customers complained about the vibrant colors, Martha briefly reconsidered her decision. Yet, she'd kept it, and now she looked on with sadness to see it defaced by a customer's rude antics.

While angered by his action, she was pleased that he managed to avoid hitting the other customers standing nearby. "Sir, leave at once. You are not wanted on these premises. Consider my previous offers revoked."

"Shove those offers up your arse."

As the door slammed behind him and the bell sounded, Martha felt several pairs of eyes on her. Knowing the best way to move forward was by addressing the drama that had just unfolded, she lifted her arms and gently waved her hands in the direction of the cashiers. "All right, folks. The show's over. Go on then."

Murmurs followed her statement, but within a few minutes, the patrons returned to their previous conversations. A few, however, glanced through

the large singular window as the disgruntled customer walked off. Rather self-consciously, Martha
wondered if the customers were talking about her
and how she handled the situation. It wasn't her
fault that the enraged customer flung their tea at
the wall. She'd kept her emotions in check. He
hadn't. It was that simple.

Without saying anything else, Martha entered
the back of the shop and, from the cleaning closet,
retrieved the items needed to clean the mess. The
last thing she needed or wanted was a customer
slipping on the residue and hurting themselves.
That would lead to serious trouble. Since his cup
was a regular size and was only filled just so, it only
took a few long wipes to remove the tea residue.
Still, cleaning up the mess took time away from
tasks that needed to be completed.

"Can you believe that?" Natalie asked as she followed Martha into the back.

"At this point in my life, I can believe practically
anything and everything," Martha responded as she
dropped the rags into a hamper.

"I swear there's nothing wrong with the milk!
I've just tested them myself this morning as we always do."

"I'm not blaming you or anyone else. Sometimes, people are just people. He probably wanted
a bit of attention."

"We're a tea shop," Natalie squealed. "Can't he

seek attention from a better, more interesting establishment?"

Martha looked on at Natalie with sympathy. Placing her right arm on Natalie's shoulder, she gave a tight squeeze and said, "It'll be alright. If this is the worst that happens to us today or this week, we'll be just fine. Do me a favor and make sure I cleaned up the mess. Then go check on the inventory. If any boxes behind the counter can be combined or broken down, please do so."

At just ten in the morning, the shop was at its full capacity. Yet, the second rush, which started around noon when people needed to step away from their desks, could cause the shop to be just as packed. Normally, it was the second rush when customers were testier and made demands like their cups being filled past the designated lines. If they were regulars, Martha allowed it, but if they were new, Martha refused. They needed to pay their dues.

Natalie pulled a face. She clearly wanted to talk more about the issue. If Martha had the time, she might have indulged in gossip, but it was Tuesday, and she needed to work on inventory. Her delivery driver was scheduled to make his regular stop today with last week's order. Still, she'd hoped to catch him before he started off that morning.

"Go on, then. We're through the worst of it."

Following the directions given to her, Natalie

sulked off. Although she couldn't see it as her back was turned, Martha smiled before sitting in front of her makeshift desk. If she opened a new shop or relocated to a bigger facility, she'd make sure there was a designated office space where she could conduct the administrative side of the business without having to worry about her employees bumping into her.

From the top desk drawer, she retrieved the clipboard that held company paperwork. Most of the teas she needed were on the order scheduled to be delivered later in the evening. It was supplies that held her interest. She felt that the last order of paper red cups had been rather flimsy. She tested a cup out upon delivery and found that she could feel the hotness of the contents more than in the previous cups. So far, a customer hadn't complained about it, but there was always a new customer ready for her to discover.

Aside from the cups, she needed more rolls of receipt paper. The rolls were getting smaller as the price was increasing. It wasn't her supplier's fault, yet all the same, she felt the need to complain to someone. It wasn't right for her to keep paying higher prices when the quality wasn't improving. For her customers' sake, it was a blessing she was so stubborn in nature, as she refused to raise the price of her tea. She was determined to hold off as long as possible. If the rent increased, well, that might be a different story.

Reviewing her list once more, Martha inhaled and exhaled. Her relationship with her supplier was standard. Her relationship with the man who delivered the goods was anything but standard. If anything, it was complicated.

Many years earlier, they'd been lovers. Gullible and naïve, she believed that they had a future together. His actions proved otherwise. Determined not to let a man turn her sour, she allowed the relationship to dissolve. From the ashes of their failed romance blossomed a secure friendship. In more than one way, Tom proved a better friend than lover.

"Hampstead Delivering Services. How may I direct your call?" A flat, nasal, feminine voice said from over the other line.

"Good morning, Sherry. It's Martha, over here at Tea Time. Who's working today, Neville or Percy?"

"I wish," Sherry said with a dramatic sigh. "Neither. It's Clarence."

"No," Martha said, lightly tapping the heels of her feet on the floor. "I can't stand him. He's such a prick."

"Who are you telling? This morning, he requested a cuppa and biscuits. Who do I look like? His maid?"

Martha gasped, "You didn't say that, did you?"

"I told him I needed to check messages and make sure the lines were clear. I reckon he got the message, as he didn't follow up. Poor old sod had to make his own tea." Sherry paused before asking, "Did you want me to patch you through to him?"

"Good heavens, no. Do you know how many times he's lectured me on my ordering? He says I'm not attuned with my customer's needs, like he would know."

Sherry clucked her tongue, "Believe me, you're not the only one." In a low voice, so the other operators couldn't overhear, Sherry said, "Last week, there was not one but two complaints filed against him."

"No," Martha said in awe, secretly pleased.

"Yes, they were from cafeterias over in Harrow. They said that not only did Clarence waste their time by offering unsolicited advice, but also refused to put their order in as requested. He didn't place an order for what they wanted but for what he thought they needed."

"What an arse."

"Exactly. He hasn't been dragged into an office yet, but it's only a matter of time. The higher-ups are tired of cleaning up his messes."

"I can imagine."

"If I can't connect you to Clarence, perhaps I can pass you through to Tom?"

Martha's throat went dry, and her heart skipped

a beat. She ought to be over the nervousness. It'd been years since she and Tom shared any form of intimacy.

"I suppose so."

"Transferring," Sherry said warmly.

"Thanks, love."

The usual beep followed. Behind the beep came a dial tone. Tom wasn't much for phone calls. He'd much rather talk to a person face to face.

"Mornin'," a deep, gruff voice sounded on the other line.

"Hullo, Tom. I need to discuss some supplies with you."

"Your order has already been packed," he snapped.

"Well, isn't it fortunate for me that I don't need it on today's order? I'm planning for next week. Now, if you don't mind, pick up your pen and ready yourself to take notes." She said the last sentence as if she were a schoolteacher addressing a rowdy bunch of students.

He chuckled and broke the character of a snobby, miserable old miser. "Oh dear, how I miss taking your phone calls."

"You see me every week."

"I know, but you know what I meant."

"So, can you help me?"

"Haven't I always been there for you, love?"

"Let's get started then," Martha said, not falling

for the flirtatious trap Tom set.

"Don't be like that, Martha. You know I have a tender heart and sensitive nature."

"For receipt paper, I want to try the G3. You do have the catalog in front of you, don't you?"

"Sure do," he answered. "G3. Hold on a second, I think this catalog is out of date. Here, G3 is a bin liner. Give me a second to find a current one. I'll set you down." With that, she heard a soft tap of the phone being placed on the desk and the sound of his heavy boots walking over a considerable distance. If she had to guess, he was probably in the warehouse. The files were in the cabinets located in the offices.

As she waited, she tapped the end of her pen against the flat, smooth surface of the desk. She wondered if he possessed the ability to truly help her. Once before, she asked him to amend her order. In the end, she'd gotten what she wanted, but it'd been a headache. Still, working with Tom was better than working with that snob Clarence. Just as her mind started to drift back to her first encounter with Clarence, a horrid, ghastly scream erupted from the front of the shop.

Without thinking twice, Martha jumped from her chair and ran through the double doors that led to the front of the shop. A sea of backs faced her. As she advanced into the crowd, she saw some male customers with their mouths gaping open while female customers were covering their mouths with their hands. A few were crying. Looking toward the counter, Martha saw a shocked Natalie close to hysterics. Brandon was holding onto her firmly as if he believed that at any moment, she would faint on the floor.

Instinctively, she wanted to ask what had happened, but given the state of the customers that filled her tea shop, she quickly determined that the best way was to find out herself. Muttering "Excuse me" and making sure not to step on anyone's feet, she made her way to the large window that looked onto the street.

As she made her way through the last line of people who stood in front of the window, she saw a pair of black leather shoes only feet away from the window. She didn't gasp or cry. Instead, she did her best not to get sick. She wanted nothing more than to take her eyes off the horrid sight in front of her, but she couldn't. A smart looking man in a well-fitted suit lay in front of the shop's window. If it were not for the puddle of blood forming on the side of his head that rested on the pavement, she'd have thought he was asleep.

A voice from the crowd asked the question on everyone's mind. "Did he jump or was he pushed?"

She had no idea. She didn't even know the name of the man. But she did know the name of the building that he was either pushed or jumped from.

The Victorian structure was called the Acheron Estate. She absolutely abhorred the building and its inhabitants. It was supposed to be residential homes back during the early reign of Queen Victoria, but the worst of bureaucracy occurred, and the developer was forced to sell off the property to individual tenants on the premise that they didn't live there but only operated their business or businesses. Or so she heard.

The building clashed horribly with those surrounding it. Martha's business operated out of a post-war building. As such, it was considered new and modern. Martha personally didn't see it that way, but if that's how her customers saw it, it was fine with her.

The Acheron Estate, with its gray stone, turrets, and narrow windows, was far from being warm and inviting. Perhaps if the individuals renting office spaces weren't so unbecoming, Martha might be able to stomach the building. During the Second World War, much of the estate endured heavy bombing. Only a quarter of the building remained. Even though it was repaired, she still desperately wanted the building demolished. But somehow, the necessary city councils decided the building held hope for better days.

"Ma'am," a frail voice called from behind.

Martha directed her attention toward the startled Natalie. In that moment, Martha knew that it was time to play to her strength. She was never the sort of person to wait and watch. She needed action. She needed to be in charge.

"Brandon," she said authoritatively. "Take Natalie to the station. Natalie, I think it's best that you go to your nan's."

"My nan's?" Natalie asked, clearly confused.

To be a decent boss, Martha needed to know her employees. Yet she didn't want to be friends with them. Doing so might give them the false impression that it was acceptable to slack off at work or to ask for favors. No, everything Martha learned about her employees she learned from the information they'd told her or that they'd told other employees, and that she overheard. She would then casually insert this information into future conversations with the employees. Normally, this triggered them to provide additional information.

From what Natalie had said in the past, Martha learned that Natalie's mum had died from breast cancer. Since her mum's death, she'd been raised primarily by her maternal grandmother Her dad didn't have the strength to raise her as a single parent. Martha could understand his plight more than he or Natalie could ever imagine.

Natalie's nan was a formidable woman who'd done a tremendous job of raising Natalie. Sure, Natalie held some characteristics of women her age, but ultimately, she was a good girl with a clever head on her shoulders. She'd yet to fall for the mistakes that others of her age had, and to Martha, that meant a lot.

"Yes, go to your nan's. You said you didn't have class for the rest of the week because you're on break, so go."

The dazed expression remained on Natalie's face, but Brandon had been jogged out of his own amazement. "Right then, Nat. Let's shove off. You look pale as a ghost."

There was hardly any color on Brandon's face, but Martha thought it best not to bring it up. Embarrassing him wouldn't help. "Go on, then, Natalie. It's best for you to go somewhere safe and secure."

Natalie opened her mouth as if she were to offer a rebuttal, but instead, she freed herself from Brandon's arm, which had been wrapped around her shoulders. She walked toward the back of the shop to where her jumper and purse were hanging on wooden pegs.

"It's best to exit in the rear," Martha advised, seeing Natalie and Brandon off.

Once they turned left at the alleyway, she returned to the front of the shop and glanced out the window. She kept her line of vision high, as she didn't want to see the corpse.

Activity was flourishing outside. Reporters with cameras flashed away. Behind the photographers were pedestrians who looked both disgusted and intrigued by the sight before them. All that was missing was the police. Had anyone called the police? Should she call the police?

The phone! She'd left Tom on the line. "Eric, it's you and me for the remainder of the day. Give me time to wrap up a call, and I'll be right out."

Eric, who didn't look the least bit interested in the scene unfolding around him, slipped his hands in his back pockets and shrugged. He was a simple boy, but to work in a tea shop, one didn't have to be Einstein.

Slightly winded, Martha snatched the phone from the desk. "Tom?"

"Where've you been?" Tom asked angrily.

Martha chose not to return the anger. Even though it wasn't her fault, she felt that technically she was in the wrong. "I'm so sorry. The most awful has just happened."

Registering the alarm in her voice, his tone changed to one of concern. "What's all going on over there?"

"Some man did a face plant on the sidewalk."

"You saw a jumper?"

"I didn't see him jump per se, but I'm having to deal with the aftermath. Wait, I think I hear the police sirens now. Took long enough. I swear the press must have at least a hundred photos of the dead man by now."

"Where did he come from?"

"I dunno. I didn't see it, but if I had to guess, I'd reckon it was the Acheron Estate. You know how horrible that place is. The people frequenting it are up to no good, mark my words."

Tom, however, did not mark her words. Instead, he hung up the phone and darted from the swiveling stool seat he'd been sitting on. Unbeknownst to Martha, while she didn't know the identity of the jumper, Tom might.

3

<u>What the Nerve</u>

A jumper at ten a.m. on a Tuesday. What a way to start a day, Detective Chief Inspector Louis Hassle mused as he exited the squad car he'd driven to the crime scene.

He winced as his feet touched the ground. They were still aching from the all-night surveillance he performed blocks away. The goal was to gather intel about a suspect group of cat burglars who weren't satisfied with just stealing expensive jewelry. They were stealing priceless family heirlooms, which they manipulated to resemble items from the royal household. A few of these items were already hitting the auction houses. Quickly identifying the dubious replications, the experts phoned the police. The experts shared how the methods used by the criminals were more advanced than they'd seen in the past. This proved Hassle's theory that not only was crime on the rise, but that criminals were also becoming more sophisticated and ruthless.

"Be gone, will you?" he commanded the gaggle of onlookers. Oh, how he hated the lot of them. People never thought twice about gawking at a crime scene, but oh, how they had reservations about aiding the police by answering questions and providing witness statements.

A police constable with a cherub-looking face waved his arms in quick, strong strokes, motioning for the onlookers to step back. Doing so gave Hassle the space he needed to enter the scene. For whatever reason, his methods were more successful than Hassle's, as the people actually moved out of the way.

Instead of giving thanks or otherwise acknowledging the constable's assistance, Hassle asked, "Why don't we have a barrier up?"

"We did, sir, but then a gust of wind blew it over. It landed rough and broke."

"And that's the only barrier Scotland Yard

owns?"

"No, sir. Anderson went to fetch the other. He should be back any minute now."

"You are?"

"Constable Martin Man, sir."

"Has the coroner arrived?"

"Not yet, sir. I'll make sure to direct him to you upon his arrival."

A sharp, sardonic response was nestled in the back of Hassle's throat, begging to be freed, yet Hassle refrained. The young chap, Martin, had done nothing to deserve the response. Still, Hassle's wrath from being tired and sore demanded that someone receive the brunt of his annoyance. Besides his sour mood, the crime scene was becoming a soup sandwich. They needed more constables working crowd control and to shoo away the photographers who were doubling by the second. Too many protocols were being breached.

"Continue to work crowd control," Hassle ordered, successfully keeping his anger and frustration at bay, if only for the moment.

"Yes, sir," Man responded with a hard nod. Turning toward the crowd, Man gave firm directions that indicated he was telling them, not asking, to move back. They did. Even from a distance, Hassle now stood away from Man and the crowd. He heard a few people call out Man's first name. *A local lad*, Hassle thought with a smirk. This might prove useful down the road.

Hassle walked over to the covered body and crouched in front of it. Delicately, as not to disturb the body and any trace evidence, he pulled back the white sheet. The man appeared to be sleeping. The congealed blood that his face rested upon told that it was a deep sleep, one that he would not be awakened from any time soon. Being only able to see one side of the face, Hassle deduced that the man must be in his early forties. His skin looked young with few wrinkles, but his hair was predominantly gray with a few streaks of dark chestnut.

Repositioning himself so that he was now looking at the back and arms of the deceased, Hassle saw that the man's hands were balled up into fists. Now, it was time to discover if the man was pushed or jumped. If there were a note explaining his actions, it'd be easy to label it as a suicide. Yet the balled-up fists and the positioning of the arms suggested he didn't choose the fall that ultimately caused his death. The side of his face that was visible showed slight puffiness under the eye, but that might be due to the fall.

He glanced up at the only building likely to be where the man could have fallen from. It stood out like a sore thumb. The building was comprised of dark gray stone, which held no warmth. The expertly crafted windows were tinted, giving the appearance of being blacked out. Weeds grew wildly around the edge of the building, as did long blades of grass that begged the question of what they were doing there. For it being the only greenery nearby, it was a dismal sight. Worse yet were splashes of unidentified liquids scattered around the lower edge of the building, as if a bloke needed to relieve himself in a hurry. Due to the obvious neglect, at least from the exterior side, the building looked as if it should have been condemned years ago.

Sure, some councils would fight tooth and nail to keep the building from being torn down, due to its alleged historic value, but where were these people when the building needed to be maintained? It wasn't their responsibility, they'd claim. It was the community's job. If Hassle had to guess, he figured the nearby businesses did their part by ignoring the building, acting as if it didn't exist. But with a deceased man lying under Hassle's nose, it did exist.

Still, in a crouched position, Hassle retrieved a notepad from his back pocket and made a note to check the building's connection to any criminal ties. There was no doubt in Hassle's mind that such a building would appeal to individuals seeking to evade police capture or to stash stolen goods until they could sell them on the market.

"Pardon me, love. I'm just going to squeeze past you," a hoarse voice wheezed as it made its way through the crowd. "Martin, what a pleasure to see you again. Has your mum's cough improved?

That's tremendous. I'm glad Dr. Gates was able to assist you. Can you point me in the direction of—wait, I see the oaf myself."

Immediately recognizing the person belonging to the voice, Hassle stood. "Good morning, Dr. Shipley. Took your time, didn't you?"

"I'll have you know that I was working on an autopsy when I received the call. I can only do so much at one time."

"That's a shame," Hassle said dryly.

"Who do we have here?"

"A deceased man, no identification on him. If I had to guess, in his early forties."

"No guessing needed. You're spot on 'bout the deceased part. You've officially earned your ranking."

"Thank you, Shipley. It took long enough. While you examine the bloke, I'm going to prowl around and gather some facts. Like the name of this bloke."

"Sounds like a good plan, if there ever was one. Listen, my assistant is cleaning up after me back at the morgue. Would you terribly mind if Man assisted in helping me loading the deceased when the time comes?"

Hassle lifted his eyes from Dr. Shipley's and surveyed the scene around. By now, the second barrier had been erected, and the crowd had significantly dispersed. Journalists continued to take photos. Of course, it'd do nicely if they got a photo or two of Scotland Yard standing next to the deceased. More police constables were on the scene. Not as many as Hassle wanted, but it was enough to make him feel the scene was more secure.

"Not a problem with me. Call him when you need him."

Hands on his hips, Hassle departed from Dr. Shipley and scanned what remained of the crowd. None wore an expression of pain and sadness from personally knowing the deceased. With his pockets empty of a wallet, the most common way to identify him was to throw him out the window. No pun intended. The people he cast his eyes on looked uninterested in the man. No crying, no sense of outrage. Just plain, simple curiosity.

"Oi, Constable French," Hassle bellowed out to the constable he'd worked with at least a dozen times before.

With long, focused strides, French advanced toward Hassle. "Sir."

"Good morning, French. Listen, I need you to gather witness statements. Pull two other constables that you trust to assist you. I want you working those closest to the body, and the other constables mingling with those in the crowd. I'll check back in before noon. Make sure you get their first and last names, as well as their phone number and address."

"Yes, sir. Bleacher and Serville are here. They're

pretty decent with this stuff."

"Good business. Work only with the crowd. I'm going to start canvassing the nearby shops," Hassle said, dismissing French with a nod.

With that underway, Hassle focused his attention on the surrounding shops and buildings. Perhaps one of these folks at one time or another had crossed paths with the deceased or at least knew something about the building opposite them. As his eyes bounced from shop window to shop window, a swinging wood sign with a teacup caught his attention. He had already consumed his standard two cups, but it wasn't against the law to have a third.

He caught Man's attention with one hand and gestured with the other where he was handing. Man nodded his confirmation. With a limited crowd to maintain, as those still present were occupied with the three officers asking questions, Man had taken a vigilant position feet away from where Dr. Shipley was examining the deceased.

A bell chimed as Hassle pushed open the front door of the tea shop. Near the counter, several people were queued for tea, while others sat at nearby tables. He never imagined that a tea shop would be so busy at that time of day, but what did he really know about tea shop businesses?

Cutting through the line, he reached the counter and addressed an earthy, middle-aged woman. The air of authority she exuded suggested that he was correct in his assumption that she was a person worth talking to.

He pulled out his credentials from his left breast pocket. "Good morning, ma'am. I'm Detective Chief Inspector Louis Hassle with Scotland Yard. I was wondering if I could talk to you about an event that transpired this morning."

She nodded in the direction of the deceased. "Him, is it?"

"Yes, ma'am. Him indeed."

"The name's Martha Strong. Let me help work down the line, and I'll be right with you."

"Of course. Take your time."

"Can I get you something while you wait?"

"A Lady Grey, if you don't mind."

Martha said she didn't mind at all. She reached around for a red cup and filled it with his desired choice of tea. "Here we are. Do be careful. I wouldn't want you to burn yourself."

He thanked her before heading off to a two-person table that was unoccupied. Watching the steam billow from the top of the cup, he wondered, on average, how many people frequented the tea shop. There were pop-ups all around London, but rarely had he ever stopped in for a cuppa.

"How's your tea, Detective?" Martha asked as she pulled the chair opposite his own a few minutes later.

"Delicious. Perfectly brewed."

Pleased with the compliment, Martha continued, "I have no idea who the man is. Before the crowd became insufferable, I managed to see half of his face. It didn't ring any bells."

Off to the races, Hassle thought. "What can you tell me about the building?"

"The building?"

"Yeah, the one across the street that could use a good swing from a wrecking ball."

Martha smiled in a conspiratorial sort of way. "You mean the Acheron Estates. It's an eyesore, isn't it? I have no love for it, but I don't have a choice. Do I?"

"What is it, and who resides in it?"

"Well," she replied slowly. "I've never been inside of it myself, and I've had scant relations with those who frequent the place. All I know is what I learned through hearsay."

"And what does the hearsay tell us?"

"It's told us that those who frequent the building are not the best lot. Before I get to that, you ought to know the history of the building, as it lends itself to its current situation. The estate was built during Queen Victoria's reign. Looks like it, don't it? Originally designed to be residential flats for those in the upper echelon of society, it fell short of expectations. Rumor had it that one of the contractors ran off with most of the funding. Imagine that," Martha paused to snort. "To make it so it wasn't a complete loss, they did what they could. They cut costs and corners. All the fancy thrills were gone. Now, in its place are boxed rooms that were then deemed as available office space."

"How many office spaces?"

"I couldn't say. I reckon not as much as before. The Luftwaffe bombs did some service by landing on much of the building. The sizeable patch of garden on the other side was where the previous part of the building once stood. Still, it's big enough to house some of the worst sort."

"How would you know they're the worst sort if you've only ever had limited contact with them?"

"You don't need to know them to know them, if you catch my drift. One of the most despicable people is a literary agent by the name of Hansel Park." She shuddered at the thought. "Just looking at him makes my skin crawl." To date, she'd only had a few interactions with Mr. Park, but there was something about the look of him that Martha knew was shifty.

Hassle wrote down the name. "Anyone else?"

"No names are coming to mind. I know of a female accountant. She's got the frizziest hair I've ever seen a woman have. She tends to clutch her suitcase as if someone's around the corner ready to snatch it from her. I hadn't seen her in a good minute, now that I think about it. Maybe a year or so. Then, there's the tailor. Well, I think he's a tailor.

He's always walking around with balled-up clothing, but he's been quiet lately. I think I saw him last Halloween. He was wearing a horrid pumpkin-inspired jumper. I think there are a few other people, but I don't know their names or what they do at the building." Martha wanted to add as an afterthought that she didn't want to know, but kept that to herself.

"I understand," Hassle said flatly. "To the best of your knowledge, has the police ever been called to the establishment?"

"No," she said almost immediately. "Granted, I'm only in the store for a certain period of time. When I've worked after hours, I've never seen anything either. Maybe the police will now take the time to investigate the place. I'm sure it's up to no good. Your lot can prove it."

Hassle glanced over his shoulder and onto the building. What was there to prove?

"You reckon any nearby businesses would know the inhabitants a little bit better?" Hassle asked before taking a sip of the tea in front of him.

"Anthony runs the dry cleaner next door, but he's not the conversational type," Martha said sourly, as if she'd tried to strike up a conversation with the business owner. "Maybe you should contact the local taxi companies. It seems that there are always taxis coming and going."

Hassle nodded appreciatively. "Back to this

Hansel Park fellow. You mentioned he was *despicable*? That's a pretty harsh assessment of someone, isn't it?"

"Easy for you to say," Martha said. "To say he gives me the creeps is an understatement. He has the darkest and shiftiest eyes I've ever seen, and he's always licking his lips. To borrow a term from my childhood, I think it's fair to say he's touched in the head."

"How do you know he's a literary agent?"

"Because he's always asking me if I like to read. He says he'll gladly trade me a book for a cuppa. I tell him to bugger off."

"When was the last time you spoke to Mr. Park?"

"More than a year. He doesn't get out much. It's odd, now that I think about it. I see him entering the facility, but I never see him leaving. Anyway, it's none of my business. All I know is that every time I see him, I do my best to avoid his path."

"Do you know what floor Mr. Park occupies?"

Martha shrugged her shoulders before glancing over at the line that was developing. "I've never stepped inside it. I wouldn't know, and I don't want to know. I've got to get back to help Eric. If you need anything else, I'll be here until six this evening."

Hassle bowed his head, "Thank you for your help, Mrs. Strong."

"It's 'Ms.' and you're welcome," she said curtly.

Finishing the tea, Hassle walked over to the large window that encompassed the long tea shop wall. It had a clear view of the building. Given the body's location, if someone within the shop had been looking out the window, they'd have seen the person fall and possibly who had pushed them. But there was no way for him to learn what customers were frequenting the shop when the man descended from the building. All he could do was hope that someone wanted to clear their conscience and call the Yard to provide any relevant information.

His right hand crumpled the red paper cup and dropped it into the nearby bin. Once again, he was on patrol. He only hoped that people were more forthcoming than Martha had speculated.

4

YOU KNOW ME

Hansel didn't know whether he should laugh or cry, so he did both simultaneously. His story was in motion. He had no idea it'd start so soon, but when the opportunity presented itself, he couldn't say no. Now that the first act was completed, all he needed was the other components to fall into place. He trusted that they would. How could they not?

From his window, which he'd pried open with random tools scattered around his office, he observed a swarm of activity occurring below. When the first set of police officers arrived at the scene of his handiwork, he squealed like a child on Christmas morning. He was slightly upset when he looked harder and discovered that there were only uniformed police officers. Where were the high-ranking ones? Those were the ones he wanted to interview. Not the low levels. Yes, it was the high-ranking ones who wore nice suits who he wanted to interview him. They'd ask the questions worth answering.

Sitting in a crouched position in front of the window, he waited—patiently waited. His time would come. Unfortunately, he paid too much attention to the police, journalists, and, of course, the deceased that he failed to notice the bigger threat coming. It was the worst sort of threat—a threat that possessed the ability to nip his story in the bud.

Just as a clean-looking gentleman departed from a shiny black vehicle whose make and model Hansel did not recognize, a hand gripped him on the shoulder and whirled him around. Hansel was neither excited nor scared. He was amused. "Hullo! It's been too long between visits!"

The face inches away from his own was very much recognizable, as it was a face he saw every morning when he brushed his teeth, trimmed his mustache, and washed his face. The face, however, wasn't as calm as his usual morning expression was. No, this face was grotesque. Rage touched every crack and crevice.

"What have you done?" the face snarled at him.

Slowly and rather dramatically, Hansel took a few steps back and used the left cuff of his jacket to wipe the specs of spit that landed on his face. "Why are you always such a grouch? Before you arrived, I was in such a giddy mood. I really was. I was thinking about how great this day turned out. I had made a new friend who asked me loads of questions. Loads! He invited me to his house. His house! Do you know that of all the authors I've interviewed, almost none have taken the time to know me? But he did!"

"Enough," the face shouted. "I don't give two shits about your new friend. Answer my question: what have you done?"

"I've put my story into motion."

"What the hell does that mean?" The face asked completely confused by the situation unfolding.

Hansel stepped toward the face. "It means my story will be told. All of it—as it should be."

"You hold on a minute now. You can't be squawking at just anyone. You've got to remember the cover."

"I'm tired of the cover," Hansel raised his arms and let them stay in the air so that resembled a scarecrow standing out in the field. "Let whatever happens happen. Like you so succinctly put it, I don't give two shits."

"Come here," the voice said in a low, menacing tone.

"No," Hansel retorted, jutting his chin up as if he were a small child refusing to take his bath.

"I said, come here."

Hansel crossed his arms against his chest. "I'm perfectly fine where I am."

"This ain't just about you. This is about us. If you don't stick to the script, I can't help you."

"Help me? Look at me!" Hansel raised his arms up once more and then spun around the room. "How have you helped me? I've been stuck in this hell for years—for over twenty-five years. I haven't touched a single blade of grass in twenty-five years!"

"Listen, old boy. You can't handle the alternative. Trust me that if I didn't do what I did, at best, you'd be caged up in some institute wearing a white jacket or buried in some prison yard. No, I found this place and did you a favor. You have what you need. You have your books. You have everything you need—more than what you deserve. Not only that, but you're making money that you have free range of."

"Free range of? What nonsense!" Hansel shouted accusatorily. "You're spending the money I'm earning for *us*! I think being locked up would have been better. What if they'd cured me?"

"There's no cure for you. There's no hope for

you. I'm all you've got."

Hansel let out a burst of laughter. "You? You think I've got you? No, no, no. You've got me!" He continued to laugh until the sides of his stomach became sore. "You keep saying this place is a better alternative. Oh, yes. What a fine alternative. But do you know what goes on here? Do you? I do! I absolutely do. I've seen the scum that calls this hellhole home. I've seen the miscreants who try to tell me what they're doing is the best for humankind. You have no idea what I've witnessed."

Hansel suddenly felt a rawness in his voice, and that was when he realized he was screaming. Using his arm to wipe the beads of sweat that started to collect on his forehead, he swayed from left to right before randomly banging on the walls around him.

"You need to calm down before someone hears you, mate."

"I want out! I want out!" Hansel shouted, placing emphasis on each vowel.

"You think this lot is a bad lot? Well, I've got some news for you—you're just like 'em. You deserved to be locked up, so I locked you up."

"How dare you compare my transgressions to those of people whom you've never met!" Hansel was more than hurt by the face's words—he was disappointed.

"Lower your tone. We can talk through this. We need to keep this between ourselves."

Hansel whirled around again. His thin lips twisted in an obscene smile. "There's no one to hear me or us," he said in a sing-song voice. "No one is left. It's only the two of us."

The face felt a cold chill. Nervously, he licked his lips. Needing to know the answer, but not wanting to hear it, he cautiously asked, "What have you done?"

"Why are you so curious now? Where have you been? Spending the money I've made—that's what you've been doing. You've kept me unchecked for too long. Over a year it's been, and now, look, an innocent man is dead." Hansel sniggered as he said, "innocent."

No, Bartholomew Jackson was far from innocent. At best, Bart was a creepy pervert that someone should have done away with years ago. Maybe Scotland Yard would give Hansel a medal for his heroic, selfless act.

"Did you push Bart to his death?"

"What if I did? What if he's the seventh person I murdered? What if he's the ninth?" Hansel gasped and covered his open mouth with his right hand before dramatically lowering it. "What if he's the eleventh person I've killed? What would you do? Ship me off to some other horrid place, so society won't know I exist? Is that your solution?"

Perspiration was now rolling down his temples and back. Despite his insistence on wiping off his forehead, the sweat continued dripping down the center of his face. The constant motion made him look like a crazed maniac swiping at invisible bugs that only he could see and feel.

"Listen, if you pull yourself together, I can get you out of this. You hear me, mate? I can get you out of here. But first, you've got to tell me what you've done. I can't help you clean up the mess if I don't know what mess you've caused." The face tried to clasp Hansel in an embrace, but Hansel jumped back, almost hitting a corner of the awkwardly shaped desk.

"You. Put. Me. In. Here." Hansel wagged his finger at the face. "Now it's time you leave. I'm expecting company."

"I'm not going anywhere."

"Yes, you are. You're returning to the hell that you crawled from."

After shouting the declaration with all the force and anger he could muster, Hansel swiftly withdrew the pistol from the hidden console of the desk and pointed it directly at the face. Without a second thought, he aimed it between the face's eyes and pulled the trigger.

The face fell onto the soiled carpet. Hansel now licked his lips, imitating the nervous habit of the recently deceased. He'd done it! He'd created another element for his story.

Returning the pistol to its location, Hansel

clapped his hands together. What he'd just committed wasn't a planned act. He'd always dreamed about aiming at the target and squeezing the trigger, but he never imagined in a hundred years that he'd actually do it. Yet, he had. He froze in place and engraved in his mind every word that had been said and every action that'd taken place. When the time came, and he was finally apprehended, he could relay how the monumental event transpired.

Once Hansel was sure he'd remembered every detail to memory, he stepped over the limp body and walked over to the corner behind the deceased. Shaking due to hunger and excitement, he grasped the arms of a sitting chair and moved it to the hallway so that the corner was now fully accessible. With his right hand, he started to tap on the wall. There was a hollow space located in the vicinity he'd just created the previous week. At the time, there was no body that he'd planned to place inside it, but creating hidden compartments within the wall had become something of a hobby for him.

A few minutes passed before Hansel discovered the hollow space. With a letter opener, he removed the eight-by-eight panel and placed it near the armchair. He then turned his attention back to the body.

"Thank goodness you were always one to care about your figure," he murmured as he half-dragged, half-rolled the body into the hole in the wall.

Working quickly, he placed the panel back over the hole, and from the bottom drawer of his desk, he retrieved a small container of plaster and an applicator trowel. As he crouched in front of the panel, he made quick and accurate motions with the hand holding the trowel. Perhaps it was the anger and resentment that he held for the deceased that caused him to patch up the wall in record time—or maybe it was because he knew company would be coming at any second.

5

<u>Wanting Home, But Settling for a Platform</u>

Finley told Hansel a white lie. There was no afternoon appointment. Aside from his appointment with Hansel, there was nothing on his calendar. Well, except for the celebratory dinner he'd been hoping to share with Eve.

Theoretically, he and Hansel could have chatted all afternoon. They could have discussed recent books they've read and enjoyed. If they so desired, they could've ventured over to the tea shop Finley passed on his way to Ainsworth Press, but he didn't want to stay. To put it bluntly and perhaps immaturely, something about Hansel gave him the creeps. Sure, he'd invited the literary agent to his home, but Finley didn't actually think Hansel would accept the offer. It was only out of courtesy, a Christian duty.

Besides, the second Hansel launched into the terms and conditions of the contract, Finley felt like a gullible fool. Deep down, he knew his ambition of being a best-selling published author was nothing more than a pipe dream.

He possessed no inclination to do business with Ainsworth Press. He'd been honest when he said he wanted his book published and wanted to go about it the smartest way. From the conferences he'd attended, he knew that literacy agencies and publishing houses wouldn't think twice about taking advantage of authors who desired literary greatness.

Eve, he mused, as he repositioned himself on the black iron bench, which he'd been sitting on for the past hour and a half. His bum was completely numb, and his legs ached, but he wasn't ready to go home. He wasn't ready to admit defeat to Eve just yet.

Not that she would mind, being such a sweet and caring girl. Never in a million years could he have imagined he'd raise such an amazingly intelligent and kind girl like Eve. Since she was a wee little girl of three, it'd been only the two of them.

He was considerably older when she was born—he was almost thirty-seven. His wife, Eve's mom, had been considerably younger at almost twenty-one. Neither of them considered the age gap odd. After all, they both wanted the same things in life: security and a family. Or at least they thought they wanted the same things. How does one really know what they want if they haven't had it before?

Perhaps it was with this logic that Finley didn't feel angry or surprised when he found his wife, Jane, sitting outside his daughter's room with her face buried in her knees.

"I can't do this," she said between sobs. "I'm tired of this."

Finley stood straight like a rod, "I can start putting Eve to bed. It's no sweat off my back."

"That's not what I mean."

Her response was muffled, yet he understood what she said and what she meant. The signs were long present. It'd been apparent to all who knew her that she deeply loved and cared for her daughter, but there was also a noticeable distance between the two. There was also the way in which she'd drift through the flat as if she weren't part of the home but someone visiting. He didn't know what to say or do, so all he did was bring her fresh-cut flowers every Thursday and tell her how pretty she looked, even when she looked like she woke up on the wrong side of the bed.

She accepted the flowers and the compliments, but she never returned any form of kindness. When the day came for him to announce that he'd finally scraped enough to buy that row house that had caught their fancy months earlier, she'd clasped her hands together. For the briefest of seconds, he believed she would either hug him in excitement. But she didn't hug or kiss him. Instead, she stayed sitting down with her hands clasped together before rising to her feet.

"I suppose I ought to get packing?"

Seeing her in the hallway completely broken down didn't throw him for a loop, but it did sadden him. If a new home that she wanted couldn't satisfy her, and the fresh-cut flowers didn't bring a smile to her lips, what else could he do? It was different back then. Maybe now, after seeing programs on the telly, he might have approached the situation differently. But that was then, and he couldn't go back.

"Do what you think is best," he said to her in a hollow voice. "I'll say only nice things about you." With that, he left her in the hallway and attended to the fussy Eve, who was demanding a bedtime story.

The next morning, she'd cleared off with their

best luggage. Later, he replaced the luggage. He never replaced her. He never stopped caring for her. He still missed her.

A few months after she left, she began to send money to the house. The letters tucked inside the envelopes were short and provided very few details about her life. The sums of money varied, but for the past few years, they'd been on the higher end. The return address was a post box. He'd given up writing her, as his attempts failed to result in a message being returned.

Eve remained none the wiser. He refused to say Jane died. No, one day, Jane might change her mind. He felt confident and secure in saying that Jane was ill. What kind of illness? The kind that is highly contagious. "She needed to leave to protect us because that's who your mum is, Eve. She's a protector. Have I ever told you about the watercolors she did when she was younger? They're stored up in the attic. Would you care to have a look? Here, hold my hand. No, a firm grasp, if you don't mind. I don't want you falling down the ladder. One strong bump to the back of your head, and I'm afraid you're a goner. No, I'm not lying. Yes, thank you. That's a fine grip."

If Eve struggled without having a mum around, she didn't show it. For the neighbor's part, they didn't whisper about Jane's sudden disappearance. Maybe they too noticed the struggle that Jane had dealt with for so long.

Being a dad was more than a joy—it was a pleasure—because as Eve matured into a young woman, he was able to share his artistic pleasures with her. It was she who, at fifteen, read the first manuscript he'd ever written. It'd been written some thirty years earlier. He dared not publish it. Yet, he felt that someone other than himself needed to see how he'd evolved as an author.

She described the story as "delightful." He doubted that was the correct word to describe it, but being only fifteen, what knowledge did she have in critiquing books? From that point on, he took it upon himself to not only share more of his stories with her but also to share his insight on why he wrote the book, why key elements were so crucial to the plot, and so forth. A few years later, Eve was able to question and, better yet, challenge him. After a short rebuke for what she called "sloppy dialogue," Finley wondered if he had done too good of a job in educating his daughter.

Although it was he who had hoped to get published, Eve constantly kept tabs on the literary agents he wrote to, seeking a partnership. By the time he reached out to the first literary agency, Decker and Nobs, he'd written seventeen novels. "Shouldn't one of them see the light of day?" she asked innocently. "Yes, it'd be nice," he answered back. But, in fact, it'd be more than nice; it'd be fantastic. What if others liked and enjoyed his writing? What vindication it would be! How marvelous to see kind words about his book in print! Surely, the negative reviews and criticisms would sting, but his skin was tough. He'd shoulder it.

Best yet was the possibility of their finances improving. Finley was not one to say no to a few pounds here and there if the money came through in ethical and decent ways. Eve deserved to be in art school, and as her dad, it was his responsibility to see that she achieved her full potential.

Would she be disappointed with his decision not to move forward with Ainsworth Press? Possibly. Most likely, however, she'd feel sad that he didn't get what he wanted—what they both knew he deserved. His books deserved to be mass-produced and to be on shelves across Britain. But the possibility might happen. If not now, later.

The disappointment he felt about his situation shifted to anger, the more he thought about his interaction with Hansel. For the life of him, he couldn't get past the oddness of that man. One could play it off as him being a creative sort of person. Weren't creative people supposed to be different? They were the ones bucking the social norms. But he wasn't that kind of odd. He didn't wear gaudy clothing or act in a ridiculous fashion to get attention. This oddness was internalized. It was almost as if he were a troubled person.

There was no way for Finley to know for sure about Hansel's diagnosis unless he asked him directly, but he'd seen men like that when he was in the war. Some such men he interacted with were during basic training. These men couldn't keep their eyes on the person they were talking to. Their eyes constantly shifted to the ground or even to a different person standing nearby. They'd release bursts of laughter, even though no one had said anything remotely funny. Sometimes, they'd laugh when it was completely silent. At first, Finley was willing to believe that the man was laughing at something he had suddenly remembered, but as it became more common, he accepted that the man was just not right. The fact that the country needed all the manpower to fight and win the war added credence that the army accepted any and everyone.

It was sympathy that refrained Finley from acting too harshly toward those men and toward Hansel. There was something not right about them, but how could they be blamed for that? He'd read newspaper articles about people being born with no limbs. He was far from being a man who knew the interworking of the different branches of science, but Finley accepted that some things in life were beyond the control of the average person.

Deep in thought about what psychological ailment might be afflicting Hansel, he didn't notice the distressed woman who sat down next to him.

Remembering his manners, he moved over his suitcase and sat straight up. The pain in his rear was
sizable, but manners were manners. He grimaced
and cleared his thoughts, lest he involuntarily react
to his thoughts and not to the events surrounding
him.

Upon landing on the edge of the bench, the
young woman hunched over and released a series
of cries. Surprised by the startling display of emotion, Finley cast an eye on the young woman to see
her knuckles bone white due to her clutching the
edge of the bench so steadfastly. In slow, steady motions, she rocked herself back and forth. It seemed
to Finley that if she rocked any faster, she'd fall off
the bench.

"There, there. I'm sure the bloke doesn't deserve all this emotion." Finley said sympathetically.
He couldn't be sure a potential lover's breakup was
the cause of her distress, but for a person her age,
he reckoned it was.

The young woman's head jerked up. "Mr.
Glover! What in the world are you doing in London?"

Taken aback, he opened his mouth and closed
it at the realization of who the speaker was. "Natalie. I'm here on business. What's all this carrying
on about? Are you ill?"

Natalie shook her head, "No, Mr. Glover. I
daresay if I were, I would be in a far better state than

I am now."

Natalie McDonald was a dear friend of Eve's. He couldn't count how many sleepovers the two had shared or how many rides to school he'd given Natalie, as they were practically next-door neighbors to the McDonald's.

Being the father that he was, he gave her two swift pats on the back. "Do you need to talk, or do you want space?"

"He's dead," she shrieked in place of answering his question.

"Who's dead?" Finley asked, alarmed.

"The man on the pavement. His skull is completely bashed in. I saw brain matter. I know I did. No one can convince me I didn't."

"Calm down, dear. No one is trying to convince you of anything. Here, our train is about to pull up. Steady now. Mind your laces. No, I'll tie them. You just stand still. Right then, come on."

Together, the two stood as people flooded out. When the stream slowed to a trickle, Finley positioned his body so that he blocked others from entering. Natalie made her way on board with him, following quickly behind. He pointed at a pair of empty seats. Catching his meaning, she plopped one nearest the handrail.

"What man are you talking about?" Finley said, reigniting the conversation.

He'd last heard that Natalie was studying

economics at university. It surprised him that such a delicate-looking girl would choose to study such a heavy topic, but she said time and again that the topic interested her.

Almost every weekend, she traveled back home, partially to see her grandmother, who filled in as a mother figure, as her real mum passed away from breast cancer, and to see Eve. Having briefly lived in London during his younger years, he knew exactly what sort of horrors she might witness.

"The man who fell from the building," Natalie said in disbelief. "He just lay there. His eyes held a most peculiar look. It was as if he were accusing me of pushing him off the building. But I'd never murder someone! Never! I especially wouldn't push someone off a building. He wasn't old or young. He still had time to enjoy life. But someone didn't want him to enjoy life any longer. They wanted him dead, Mr. Glover."

To Finley, she spoke as if he personally knew the man and building she was referring to, but he didn't. With her distress increasing as she spoke, he contemplated shifting the conversation to a different topic, yet she seemed too eager to discuss the occurrence, and he couldn't help but be interested in the tragedy. He'd never heard of someone jumping off a building.

"Natalie, I need you to breathe in and out. Thatta a girl. Now, let's start at the beginning. I have not the slightest clue as to what you are talking about. I wish to help you, but I need more details."

"I was at the shop." Finley knew she worked at a small tea shop. The little money she earned went to makeup and jewelry. When visiting, Natalie regaled Eve with stories about rude customers and, sometimes, even ruder coworkers. She spoke kindly of the shop manager, Ms. Strong.

"I'd been asked to replenish the paper cups. As I was taking the plastic wrap off the cups, I heard a loud gasp from right behind me. I turned around to see what the commotion was about. I thought perhaps the customer dropped hot tea on themselves. You know, that happens. Not often, but still. Anyway, that's when I saw this dark blue blur falling from the sky. At first, I thought it was a pile of clothes. You see, there's a couple that lives above the shop. Sometimes, they have lovers' quarrels. Nancy, that's the woman's name, will throw John's, that's the man's name, belongings out the window. Sometimes, it's his university books; other times, it might be his cricket gear. I thought, this time, it was a pile of his favorite clothes. But that went away when I heard the sound of the blur making contact with the ground." Natalie shuddered and gripped the bottom of her seat as if she feared falling off.

"Natalie, I'm so sorry. That's horrific. I wish you hadn't seen that."

"Me too. When I glanced down, it wasn't that bad. That was until I saw him blink. He blinked! His eyes looked right in my direction."

Knowing more about death than he'd ever wanted to, he knew that this mystery man most likely died upon impact. If he were, in fact, a blur as Natalie described, then he would have had to fall from a considerable distance. No sooner had he drawn his conclusions had Finley wondered about what building the man fell from. Before asking, he felt the need to help resolve some of the crises she was currently feeling.

"Natalie," he said, softly squeezing her hand, "you've seen something horrid. It might take a week, a month, or even a year to move on, but you will move on. There is a place for everyone in the hereafter."

"My boss said I needed to go to Nan's because Nan can take good care of me. I think Nan will say exactly what you just said, though."

"Great minds think alike," Finley chuckled.

"Mr. Glover," Natalie quietly admonished, "here I was thinking you were the modest sort."

"All men have egos, my dear."

"I wonder if he did."

"Who?"

"The dead man. I wonder if some sort of great sadness caused him to jump. Last semester, a young woman that I took advanced calculus with overdosed on pills. I saw her parents when they came to collect her belongings. They looked gutted." Natalie closed her eyes. All the color drained from her face. The wheels in her mind continued to turn. Then, without much effort, she muttered, almost to herself, "But, what if he didn't jump? What if someone pushed him?"

"Come now, it does us no good to speculate," Finley admonished.

"I know you're interested. You have to be! Eve's told me about all the books you've written. I've even read two, maybe three. You have a talent."

Flustered at not knowing she'd been privy to his creative endeavors, Finley cleared his throat and returned to his earlier sentiment. "If there's anything suspicious about his death, the police will investigate. It's not our place to judge or gossip."

Before the last few words left his mouth, Natalie turned to face him. Her eyes were wide with excitement and wonder, "Mr. Glover, think about it. With all the details I've given you, it must indicate murder."

"You've given me no details."

"I'm sure I have," Natalie said, her voice trailing off. "Alright, then. He was dressed well. His suit fit him perfectly. People down on their luck hardly ever dress nicely. His hair, from what I could see, was maintained. Not long or unruly. So, we know he was keeping up appearances."

"Appearances aren't enough. We need to know about his personal background. What if he was having a bad day? What if he'd just been let go from his place of employment?"

Natalie snapped her fingers, "See, I knew you'd be interested. What if the murder was competitive in nature? Maybe he was a popular, successful salesman, and a rival sought to knock him off, so he could take his position?"

While Finley actively partook in the conversation, he held mixed feelings about talking about such a horrid event. The loved ones of the deceased must be devastated by the news. Yet, the more she talked, the more he was reeled in. Natalie, too, was drawn to the facts and details that she no longer saw the dead man's body sprawled out on the pavement.

"How about we hop off to get some newspapers?" Natalie suggested. "Do you think they've picked up on this by now?"

"The police hardly have time to investigate. Journalists need facts to work with. If they conjecture too boldly, they can lose their credibility or, even worse, end up in court," Finley lightly scolded.

"Do you think the evening television news will have something about the murders?"

"It's possible."

"Can I have dinner with you and Eve? Nan

doesn't like watching the evening news. She calls it 'trash,' but I don't think it is. Do you?" Natalie asked eagerly.

"It has its moments, I suppose," Finley said neutrally.

"Is this inspiring you? You know, for a new story?"

"Well," he sputtered, "I've only heard of the event. To date, I've yet to be inspired by a murder."

"That doesn't mean you won't. What if I get inspired to write a story? Would I be imposing?"

Finley grabbed her left hand. "Darling, anyone and everyone should write whatever comes to them. Should this result in you writing a story, I shall read the story."

She returned his squeeze before casting her eyes downward. She, too, was lost in thought. Selfishly, Finley wondered if this would be the distraction that he needed. It wouldn't soften the blow of not getting the contract, but it might be something worthwhile to tell her.

No, he thought to himself. He didn't want Eve subjected to such a grisly topic. She was such a soft young woman. He was grateful that, unlike others her age, she chose to remain in the village and not venture off into a big city. She'd survive, but he didn't want her to have any battle scars.

6

A Raincheck for Bad Days

Hassle stepped three feet into the entrance lobby of the Acheron Estate and almost immediately fought the strong urge to vacate the premises. The squalor that greeted him was unimaginable. The geometric red and gold wallpaper that was splattered with dark green specs was starting to peel off in the corners. The once-light beige carpet was now dark and soiled with streaks of mud and other questionable brown stains. The smell of stale cigarette smoke hung in the room as if every citizen in London had piled into the room and lit one up.

His eyes scanned the dimly lit room to find signs indicating the location of a lift. Not seeing an arrow or sign, he advanced down the first corridor on his left. Sure enough, across a flight of stairs directly behind him, he saw a sliver of brass gold. He cautiously walked over. With every few steps, he expected some unsavory person to jump out and give him a fright.

When first constructed some forty years ago, the lift must have looked modern and sleek, but currently, it looked nothing short of a death trap. Pulling the cage door open, a series of squeaks sounded from the hinges. At once, he began to doubt the lift's functionality. Inside the lift, his eyes looked above the floor-level buttons where the inspector's card indicated when the last inspection was to have occurred. There was no inspection card. Hassle's stomach turned.

With a long stride, he exited the lift. He left the door open. "Fine then," he murmured to himself. He'd trek it up the stairs. Approaching the staircase, he withdrew a small pocket torch he always carried with him. Early in his tenure as copper, he'd learned that having a light on oneself was one of the best ways to guarantee safety and security.

From the posting outside the front door, he learned that his person of interest, Hansel Park, the person whom Martha Strong thought so strongly of, was on the third floor. Of course, he was. An athlete in his younger days, Hassle routinely made an attempt to keep up his muscle mass, if only for vanity's sake. He'd still run the occasional marathon with the younger men on the force. Yet, having to take several flights of stairs after the dismal night and morning caused his knees to throb and lungs to ache.

On the second flight of stairs, he paused and pressed his hand against the wall for support. At feeling something sticky and wet, he retracted his hand. In the somewhat darkness, he retrieved the handkerchief from his breast pocket. He'd hate to soil it with the unknown substance, but he dared not wipe whatever it was on his pant leg. This Hansel Park had better be in his office. If he wasn't, Hassle vowed to dispatch as many officers as he had at his disposal to find the man. He threw the crumpled handkerchief in the corner and focused on the remaining distance.

Breathing through his mouth as his nose refused to inhale the urine-like smells that surrounded him, he became aware of how quiet his surroundings were. In a building, no matter the sort, there was always movement of some kind. People talking, laughing, moving. But apparently not in this building. Silence accompanied the smells of human bile and cigarette smoke.

With his right hand on the railing of the third

floor, he made a personal promise to himself to call the council and have this building condemned. He was quite certain that the dark brown, black, and light purple specs on the ceiling were mold. The geometric wallpaper that started on the ground floor carried throughout the building. Now, it looked less preserved, with pieces torn and sections slashed. The markings suggest that those who took the same steps as Hassle had grown restless during the journey to their designated floor. The light fixtures that were still present were hanging on to the walls for dear life. On more than one, copper wires were exposed. Each lightbulb cast a different shade of light, indicating a different wattage. Some looked bright as if they were just installed, while others flickered, warning that they were mere minutes away from giving away.

Despite the strong feeling of disdain, Hassle did not cast judgment or wonder how people voluntarily lived in such squalid conditions. The fact of the matter was that people no longer surprised him, even if their actions appalled him.

When he entered the field of law enforcement, he brought with him a certain air of naivety. All young coppers of his generation did. A few kept the mindset throughout their career. They continued to think that deep down, people were good and righteous. On occasion, they—the police—encountered pure evil at its worst, but the majority of the people were good. It was simple, really; they helped the good and locked up the bad.

This level of optimism abandoned Hassle eight months into his career. He had responded to a distress call. A distraught woman ran down a police officer walking the beat. This was during the early years of the war when officers were few and far between. With much persistence, she managed to persuade the officer to follow her to her neighbor's flat. There, the officer found blood splattered throughout the small, cramped living quarters.

Lying on the kitchen floor, clutching her stomach, was a young woman, no older than twenty-one. The stomach she clutched clearly had been split open by several blows from a sharp axe. There was no color in her face, and her pulse was low and unsteady. If she hadn't been whispering, "Why?" the officer would have thought her dead.

Beyond petrified, the officer leaned out the window and shouted for any nearby coppers to join him. His strong, deep voice called out codes that other trained officers were supposed to know by heart. Hassle, who was just starting his shift for the day, heard the calls.

He groaned and hypothesized as to what started the altercation. From the shouting being done by the first officer, Hassle gathered that a woman was seriously injured and required medical attention. With emotions such as fear running high, it wasn't uncommon for dubious relations to start. In all likelihood, a romantic or even domestic affair turned sour. Perhaps the woman stepped out on the man or had backtalked him. Nowadays, the possibilities seem endless.

Pushing all speculation and judgment aside, Hassle responded to the call. With a quick pace, he ran the few blocks over. Once he was close, he shouted back to the officer and provided his police number.

Bounding up the steps, Hassle observed that a good majority of the doors were either cracked open so that the residents could hear the commotion or were wide open so they could both hear and see the action transpiring. While he felt eyes on his back, he felt grateful that no one had felt the nerve to ask him any questions.

"Be careful. It ain't pretty in here," the first officer half greeted, half warned, with a slight tremble in his voice.

It never was.

Immediately, after entering the threshold of the flat, the other officer stood in front of, the hairs on the back of Hassle's neck raised while goosebumps formed on his forearms. Something wasn't right. Hassle scanned the cramped flat furnished with thrifted pieces of furniture. His eyes instinctively went to the corners and behind the larger pieces of furniture.

"How long do you think until medical gets here?" The first responding officer asked, distracting Hassle from his search.

"I dunno. I think I saw an ambulance on the same street that I started off on, but I'm not sure. Hassle," Hassle extended his hand, which the other officer took and shook with a firm grip.

"Bradly. I ain't never seen anything like this."

"Where is she?"

Bradly nodded to the kitchen. Together, the two men entered the scene. From the threshold, Hassle saw that Bradly had placed a wet rag on the victim's forehead. A metallic smell filled Hassle's nostrils, causing the back of his mouth to go dry.

"I didn't know what else to do," Bradly offered.

Hassle nodded.

"You think she'll make it?" Bradly questioned.

Examining the vast amount of blood that pooled around the victim's body, Hassle knew the answer, but he didn't want to say it out loud, in case the victim, who was slipping in and out of consciousness, overheard him. Instead, he reached toward the secondhand table and removed the maroon tablecloth that draped it. Although tattered with small burn marks and grease stains, it'd serve his purpose.

Careful not to jostle the body too much and cause the victim more pain, Hassle delicately slid the tablecloth under her, pulled the ends of the tablecloth upwards towards him, and then tightly knotted it over the multiple slashes. It was the only way he knew how to stop the bleeding.

"There, there, dear," he said softly as he stroked a few strands of auburn hair behind her ears. "The ambulance is coming for you. They're gonna stitch you up and make you better. Can you hear me? Come on, love. You've gotta stay with me. Squeeze my hand. That's a girl. Squeeze it hard. Look at you! Strength of an ox, you have. Can you tell me who did this to you?"

It came out faint, but it came out: "Christopher."

"Christopher?" Taking his eyes off her pale green eyes, he glanced down at her hand. On her left ring finger was a small diamond ring. "Is he your husband?"

Her head jerked as if to nod. "No more babies."

"Stay with me, love. Come now, why aren't you squeezing my hand? I need you to squeeze my hand."

His question was answered by silence. He felt the stinging of tears form in the back of his eyes, but he willed them away. Now wasn't the time. When he was back at his own flat, he could relieve the sadness that was slowly consuming him, but not now. Not in front of the neighbors who were now gathered outside. Not in front of the officer who was cursing the brute who did this to her.

Had it not been for the loud thuds of footsteps on the floor behind him, which he presumed to be the paramedics, Hassle would have continued to hold the now-deceased victim's hand. Turning around so that he could direct the paramedics to the body, he found a man aged roughly twenty-five with a large amber bottle in his hand. The young man looked at Bradly, then Hassle, before turning away as if to run.

An anger, which at that point he'd never felt before, consumed him. No, this monster wasn't getting away with what he'd done. He wasn't going to spend one more moment enjoying the sun on his skin or the wind on his back.

Hassle jumped from the crouched position he'd been in. With his arms outstretched, he focused his attention on the young man's neck. Instantly, his hands were around the fellow's throat. He jerked him back and forth until he was sure he'd dizzied him. Moving his dominant hand to the back of the fellow's head, he clumped a gaggle of unkempt brown hair and began slamming it against a door frame. A stream of blood ricocheted off the door frame against the wall.

Bradley, who was considerably bigger and stronger than Hassle and the suspected perpetrator, pulled Hassle off the fellow.

"Are you Christopher?" Hassle shouted. "Are you the pathetic entity that is Christopher? Is that what you enjoy doing—attacking a pregnant woman?"

"There, come now. Let the court have 'em," Bradley grunted as he struggled to control the now-flailing Hassle.

The events that transpired after Bradly consoled him were a blur. He remembered the paramedics coming. He remembered his superiors reprimanding him. He remembered drinking one too many that night. He remembered the perpetrator's full name as Christopher Adam Homes. He remembered the jury acquitting Christopher on the grounds of lack of evidence. The police failed to locate the axe. He remembered that a few months later, Christopher's body was retrieved from the River Thames. The coroner ruled it a suicide. Hassle didn't remember the person who called the body into the police.

Jumping back into the present, he remembered that his focus was on speaking to Mr. Hansel Park. Ms. Strong had said that this Mr. Park was a literary agent. How would a writer trust a literary agent who worked in such conditions?

Reaching his destination, Hassle breathed a sigh of relief. He raised his right hand and knocked on the faded brown door in rapid succession. Silence followed. No movement of feet or the sound of furniture being pushed back.

With lost patience, Hassle pounded on the

door, "I'm DCI Louis Hassle with Scotland Yard. I wish to speak to you about an incident that transpired early this morning. This will only be a brief interview."

Seconds passed. Then minutes.

Hassle pounded again. "Open up."

"Coming," a muffled voice called from behind the door.

Hassle closed his eyes and counted to ten before opening them, "I haven't got all day. Open this door at once."

"I understand. Just one more minute. I was in the middle of something, you see."

Using full force, Hassle pounded on the door again. This time, the doorframe rattled.

Seconds after his hand dropped to his side, the door swung open. Standing on the other side of him was a decent-looking man dressed rather smartly. His suit was a dark steel gray, which Hassle hardly saw anymore. Come to think of it, the cut was a bit dated as well. He hadn't seen long pockets on a suit in some time.

"Hansel Park?"

"Good morning, or should I say good afternoon, Detective Chief Inspector Louis Hassle," Mr. Park responded in a crisp tone.

"I need you to answer questions pertaining to an event that transpired earlier this morning. May I come in?"

"But of course, detective." Hansel stepped aside, and Hassle entered.

Upon entering the room, Hassle gritted his teeth. The stuffiness of this room was as overbearing as the putrefied smells that lingered on Mr. Park's suit. What in God's name was wrong with this building?

"Please, sit down," Hansel was saying. "Care for a cup of tea? I can put on the kettle. I have a little dinette just around the corner."

Hassle shook his head. He dared not put anything from this building on his lips or in his mouth. "I'm not interested in tea, just information."

"Right then. Let's crack on, shall we?"

Ignoring the dilapidated bookcases that surrounded him and the impending doom that would occur should they fall onto him, Hassle retrieved his notepad and began his inquiry.

"Where were you this morning between eight and ten a.m.?"

Hansel's eyebrows furrowed together, "I've been here all morning, and I haven't seen anything out of the ordinary. Perhaps you have the wrong building?"

"No, Mr. Park. I have the correct building. The event didn't occur within the building but rather outside."

"I see. Please, call me Hansel."

"Before we continue, I think it's best we open

some windows." Hassle suggested, as his eyes settled on a soft orange ceramic ashtray.

Hansel shook his head, "I think we ought to leave them closed. Bugs, you know. And the outside smells. Just last week, a ghastly cloud of petrol blew into the flat. It took days for the smell to dissipate."

"Nonsense. You're too high up," Hassle retorted gruffly, as he stood from the chair. He also wanted to add that the smell of petrol would be a welcome relief to the current smell of the room. With considerable strength, he opened the window to the left of Hansel. He eyed the right window and observed nails in the panes. "Why are your windows nailed shut?"

"I believe I'm allowed to do what I want in my own flat. It's not illegal to have windows nailed shut."

"It's considered a fire hazard."

Hansel released a dark laugh, "Jumping from this high to escape a fire would be considered safe?"

"In the event of an emergency, you can open the window and call for help. Phone lines can get damaged during a fire."

"I'll look into it," Hansel said neutrally.

"Now then, back to the questions at hand. How long have you been occupying this office space?"

"How is that relevant?"

"Answer the question. Believe, Mr. Park, I've

been in this business long enough to know what questions are relevant and which ones are not."

A strong feeling of exhaustion was settling behind the back of Hassle's eyes. He wanted sleep and a good English breakfast. Dealing with a pompous prick who looked as if he enjoyed toying with people was never Hassle's specialty. In his current condition, it might be the match that lit the fuse to his temper erupting.

"Hansel. Call me Hansel. I've been here for roughly twenty-seven years."

"You say it as if it were a prison sentence," Hassle said dryly.

"Life is a prison sentence if one isn't living how they want."

"I see. Do you know the other occupants of the building?"

Hansel shrugged his shoulders. "My path has crossed with others' paths. For the most part, however, I stick to my office and my space. I try not to get caught up in other people's affairs."

"Always a wise decision. Are you able to provide any names of the people who've worked here?"

Clucking his tongue in rapid succession before exhaling an overdramatic sigh, Hansel withdrew a long, slender notepad from the top right drawer of his desk. Grabbing a ballpoint pen, he started to scratch the surface of the pad of paper with the end of the pen. Every so often, he frowned and drew a thin line through something he'd written. Minutes passed before Hansel abruptly put the pen down and extended the sheet of paper to Hassle.

"Do you have a personal connection to these people?"

"They have a history with the premise."

Growing tired of Hansel's answers, Hassle folded the note in half and tucked it into a pocket without so much as looking at the names Hansel provided. "Right, then. So, back to this morning. Nothing odd or unusual occurred?"

"I daresay no. It was a rather average morning. My day began at seven a.m. sharp. I made some telephone calls and marked a few up-and-coming meetings on my calendar. Once I completed those tasks, I readied myself for a meeting with an author I'm hoping to sign."

"The author's name?"

"Finley Glover. He's a rather likeable chap. We had a lively discussion."

"His address?"

"I'm not sure off-hand, but once I'm able to locate it, I'll make sure to forward it to Scotland Yard."

"What did you do after the meeting?"

"I did what I always do between clients or when I have downtime: I picked up a book and read. Here," Hansel extended a red paperback book to

Hassle, who did his best to mask the disgust he felt. From where Hassle sat, he could see smudge marks of grease.

"I'm not much of a reader myself."

"Suit yourself," Hansel said as he plopped the book on the edge of the desk.

"Let me get this correct: between the meeting you had this morning and your impromptu reading session, no strange occurrences transpired?"

"Correct," Hansel confirmed with an affirmative nod.

"No arguments? No shouting?"

"Well, as you saw for yourself, I prefer to keep my windows closed. If there had been any shouting or arguing of sorts, I would not have heard it. Would I've?"

Now that the subject of windows was mentioned again, Hassle noticed the midafternoon breeze had done wonders for the cramped office. A strong stench of cigar smoke remained, but smells of bakeries and perfumes wafed in, despite the office being on a high floor.

"Are there any people who occupy this building that you might consider to be a danger?"

Hansel refrained from the laughter that threatened to erupt. He stopped the chuckle but did a poor job of keeping his face from contorting.

"Are you alright?" Hassle asked, disturbed by the spectacle.

"Yes. Please excuse me. I can't help but think that's a bizarre question. I've already made it clear that I've never taken the time to know those who occupy the building, yet you're continuing to assume I do."

"Perhaps I believe you're lying? Maybe you're trying to pull wool over my eyes?" Hassle said the words in a nonchalant fashion secretly hoping that they would leave their mark on Hansel.

They did. Hansel leaned back in his seat and rested his hands on the arms of the chair. "I can see that this is an important case, as you're implying a serious incident has occurred. While you haven't told me many details regarding its nature, you're here from Scotland Yard; therefore, it must be serious. Deadly, perhaps?. If that's the case, then I suppose it's only right to share my little secret with you."

Hassle's right eyebrow raised at hearing the word "secret."

"Mr. Park, this isn't a game," Hassle said straight-faced. "A *murder* brought me here. Now's not the time to decide what information you have a right to divulge and what information you wish to retain."

"I agree with you a hundred percent," Hansel said, lifting his hands in the air as if to surrender. "That is why I'm going to share with you my medical condition: I have not left this room in over twenty-seven years. If you're as astute as I think you are, you would know by now a brief history of the Acheron Estate. It was meant to be flats for the rich, blah, blah, blah. But what few people fail to realize is that the flats remained as flats. There are no dedicated offices. Sure, there are people like me who run their businesses out of their flats. Overall, these are flats that people live in. People have always lived here despite what the rumors and speculation say." He paused before directing Hassle to follow him.

Hassle did, reluctantly. With every step Hassle took, he tried to suppress the growing sense of discomfort within him. The man before him was definitely an odd sort, but how odd?

"You see this decorative wall hanging? It masks a door. It leads to a kitchenette area where I prepare and cook my meals. I mentioned it earlier."

Hansel repositioned a tapestry of medieval knights gathered at a round table and pulled on a ceiling lamp string to illuminate the tight area he was describing. From his position, Hassle saw a gray sink and a spot of counter space. He deduced that Hansel must not have been the greatest cook. He couldn't see how anyone could prepare more than a sandwich in such a small space.

Crossing the room, Hansel pushed on a blank space in the wall. Hassle expected nothing to happen, but he was wrong. A slender panel moved, exposing a metal-framed bed. "I sleep here when I'm able to. I'm afraid insomnia has taken its toll on my mind."

While Hansel prattled on about the comforts of his home and office, Hassle concentrated on the information presented by Hansel. He claimed not to have left his office in over twenty-seven years because of a medical condition. But hadn't Ms. Strong said that she'd crossed him on the street? Between Ms. Strong and Hansel, if he had to choose who was more prone to honesty, he'd choose Ms. Strong.

"Why can't you leave?" Hassle interjected, cutting Hansel off mid-sentence.

"Come again?" Hansel stammered.

"You said you can't leave. Why? Is it the phobia of being outside? Are you allergic to grass?"

"Allergic to grass? How silly!" Hansel exclaimed with a forced laugh before deciding the time was right to ask the question burning in his mind. "Are you good at your job, Detective Hassle?"

Hassle's body stiffened at the question and at how Hansel's eyes suddenly narrowed. Over the years, he'd been asked many questions during interrogation and when collecting witness statements. Surprisingly, the question Hansel presented was rarely asked.

"Yes," Hassle said slowly but firmly.

"How many cases have you solved?"

"While I'm flattered by your interest in my

career, I'm here to discuss the event that transpired earlier this morning. Can anyone vouch that you permanently reside within the Acheron Estate?" Hassle said cuttingly. He didn't need or want Hansel's deflection. He wanted his questions answered so he could leave the godforsaken building.

Hansel sidestepped the question, "Out of all the murderers you've caught, who's your favorite? I'm assuming there's one devilishly, cold-hearted murderer that lingers in the recesses of your memory? What did they do to earn the top spot? How horrific were their crimes?"

The hardened, reserved lines that had previously rested on Hansel's face were gone. An almost boyish, amused expression took its place.

Hassle snapped his notepad closed. "There are two options for you to pursue: you answer my questions, or I take you to Scotland Yard and book you for hindering a police investigation. Which is it?"

"Neither," Hansel said with a nonchalant shrug. "What a shame. It seems that all your associates have left you behind."

"Come again?"

"All the police cars are gone. Look! The ambulance is driving away with poor Bartholmew."

Hassle's discomfort transcended to confusion. "You know the victim?"

"Yes. I know the name of the victim, and I know

why he met his untimely death. Unfortunately, you never will. You've disappointed me, Louis. Can I call you that? Are we on those terms yet? We might as well be. After all, I'm the last person you're going to see alive."

Hassle retained his composure. In a swift motion, as Hansel whirled around, both men retrieved a weapon from their breast pocket. For Hassle, it was the service weapon that his brother had bequeathed to him. Hansel withdrew a pistol. In a matter of seconds, after Hansel had uttered the word "alive," two loud popping noises sounded in the office. One man hit the ground, while the other fell back against the wall before sliding onto the floor.

7

HOME IS WHERE THE HEART IS

By the time Natalie and Finley pulled into their re-
spective station, sheets of rain engulfed their view.
Finley's heart sank. He wasn't in the mood to wait
out any storm. He desperately wanted to get home
to his daughter. Given the time, Eve might have
started preparing her favorite lunch of grilled
cheese sandwiches and tomato soup.

"You know, I could always call Nan to come
pick us up? Unlike other older ladies, she doesn't
mind driving in such horrible weather," Natalie

said, almost bragging.

The idea didn't sound awful to Finley, but he personally didn't want to see Daphine, Natalie's nan, driving in such weather. "I think it's best to stick it out a little bit. I'm sure it'll let up sooner than later."

"Maybe thirty minutes, but no longer. My stomach's growling. I haven't had anything to eat."

"Right. I'm afraid we're in the same boat there. How about I buy us a bag of crisps and a nice hot cuppa?"

Natalie's face brightened at the thought of crisps. "That would be great. Thank you so much!"

He directed Natalie to an empty bench, as all the others were taken by those who were also riding out the storm. Once she was seated, he scanned the area to make sure no suspicious people were lurking about and walked over to the station's mini shop. During their discussion on the train, the two had talked at great length about murderers and horrid people in general. Each was aware of the infamous trials and convictions that plagued British history.

As a young woman, Natalie was more interested in the present. He preferred the highwaymen who terrorized the rich. Unlike Natalie, he hadn't kept up with the most scandalous murder trials of the day. An avid newspaper reader, he made sure to keep up with current events, so he knew about some murders, but not to the extent that Natalie did. She claimed rather indignantly that as an independent woman living in the nation's capital, she needed to know how murderers thought. Getting inside their mind would help determine how not to fall susceptible to them.

Finley didn't agree with her reasoning in the slightest, but he was impressed and relieved to know that she put such serious emphasis on her well-being and safety. The women in his office were a few years older than Natalie, but lived a more carefree lifestyle. More than once, he'd heard a woman leaving her door unlocked, so her husband wouldn't wake her up with his keys when he got home after a late-night shift.

"Hello there, how may I help you?" a pleasant-looking woman greeted him, her big gray bun bobbing up and down as she nodded.

"Good day. I would like two bags of crisps, original flavor, two of those packaged pastries, and two cups of tea."

After giving Finley his total and accepting the amount due, she turned around, grabbed a brown paper bag, and gently placed the crisps and pastries inside.

"Mind yourself. I don't want you to go burning yourself," she cautioned eyeing the cups of tea.

"Yes, ma'am. Will do."

With the paper bag tucked under his right arm

and the two paper cups held firmly in his hands, he walked over to the bench and offered Natalie tea. As she wrapped a hand around the cup, his eyes glanced up out the window. The rain had not let up in the slightest. Now, bolts of lightning illuminated the sky.

"Thank you so much. I really do appreciate it. You've always been the most generous person. Is one of these pastries for me?" Natalie asked as she rummaged through the brown paper bag.

"It is, and as is one bag of crisps."

In silence, the two munched on the cream cheese pastries and chips. Finley popped the last bit of pastry into his mouth and wished he'd chosen the cherry flavor instead. Oh, well. Perhaps if he asked nicely enough, Eve would make him some cherry scones or something of the like. She was such a talented baker.

"What are you going to tell Eve?"

Jerked from his thoughts about cherry scones, he cast his gaze in Natalie's direction. Did she know about his meeting with Ainsworth Press? He'd sworn Eve to secrecy. She was not one for breaking a secret, no matter how big or small it might be.

"Come again?"

"What are you going to tell Eve about the jumper? Are you going to tell her he was pushed or jumped?"

"Oh, that. I don't think I'll bring it up to Eve,

and I hope you won't either."

"But I have to tell her! She'd be gutted if I didn't."

"You know as well as I do that Eve doesn't like anything grim. A person falling to their death would greatly upset her." He spoke gently but added a hint of firmness to his voice so that Natalie got the impression his view could not be changed.

Natalie grew quiet. After a few moments, when a clap of thunder erupted from the steel gray sky, she turned to him, "I suppose this could be our little secret?"

Finley chuckled. He didn't like the thought of him sharing any sort of a secret with a person the same age as his daughter, even if he had known her since she was a small girl wearing plats. "I'll tell you what, when more information is brought forth on the matter, we can discuss what's transpired."

Believing that it could take days or weeks for the police to make a discovery in the case, he thought his offer was fair. Besides, she was a young person. Chances were that her interest in the case would have evaporated. A movie, book, song, or young lad would take her fancy and lead her interests in a different direction.

"Has this inspired you to write? Maybe you'd write a novel about a deranged killer stalking the streets of London?" She'd asked earlier, but this time, she thought with the passing of time, he'd provide her with a different answer.

"There are enough of those books already. No, I think I'll stick to my preferred genre. Tell me, do you enjoy reading?"

Natalie nodded, "I like reading. I try to find the time. But you know, now that I'm at university, I have to buckle down and prioritize my studies. When my brain feels like it's caving in, I take a breather and pick up a mystery."

"Mysteries? I enjoy a good mystery myself. Would you recommend any particular one?"

Natalie looked as if she were ready to answer her question when the sound of shuffling feet sounded through the station. Both of them glanced out the nearby window and found that it was no longer raining. Seeing their opportunity, the two got to their feet and joined the crowd vacating the station. Finley practically threw the crumpled-up paperback into the nearest bin.

A yard away from the station, Natalie asked, "How long do you think we have before the sky lets up again?"

Finley, who wasn't running but was taking quick, long strides, shrugged his shoulders. "I'm not sure. But our homes are just around the corner. I'll be glad to get there. Hop to, young lady."

In unison, Natalie and Finley took long strides to the tree line that separated their homes from the main road. Only when their feet hit the pavement did they slow their pace.

As if sensing his approach, the front door swung open. There stood Eve with a wide smile on her face. With her eyes firmly planted on her father, she asked, "Are we a signed author?"

"We are considering the offer presented to us by Ainsworth Press," Finley said with a forced smile.

Eve took Finley's suitcase and overcoat. After setting them on the stand, she acknowledged her old friend with a hug and a quick peck on her right cheek. "Great to see you, Nat."

"Same, Eve. I've missed you terribly."

"Why are we thinking it over?" Eve asked, turning to Finley.

"We can't just put all our eggs in one basket, darling. We need to see our other options."

"I guess," Eve said, not so certain of Finley's approach. "I'll go on and warm up the kettle." Without further ado, she left Natalie and Finley in the parlor. From inside the kitchen, over the sound of the running tap, she called out, "You've been gone for so long. I started to think you were having a celebratory pint."

"Come now," Finley gently admonished. Sitting in his favorite plaid recliner, Finley felt a feeling of warmth and comfort engulf him like a favorite blanket. "If I were to celebrate, I would surely have you tag along."

"You mean *when.*" Seeing the confused look on Finley's face, Eve clarified, "When you sign a literary contract, you and I will celebrate. And we will celebrate in a big style. Natalie, too!"

"Absolutely! I shall bake the most fabulous cake," Natalie said brightly.

Eve affectionately patted her dad's shoulder and then entered the kitchen. From the parlor room, the sound of mugs being removed from the cupboards could be heard. Always being a quiet person by nature, Eve closed the cupboard's door in a swift but gentle manner. "Nat, did you want your usual herbal tea?"

"Yes, please."

"And dad, did you want an Earl Grey?"

"If you please."

With all attendees comfortably settled in the parlor room, Eve felt it was only right to carry on the conversation. "So, tell me. What was Mr. Ainsworth like?"

"Mr. Park, dear. His name is Hansel Park. He runs Ainsworth Press."

"Hansel? I don't believe I've ever met anyone named Hansel. Isn't that a Dutch name?"

Finley shrugged his shoulders, "It could be for all I know."

"Wait a second," Natalie muttered with the gears in her head slowly churning. "You visited the Acheron Estate?"

"Yes, earlier this morning. Around nine. I left shortly before ten."

The recognition of the timeline caused Natalie to choke on her tea. "Then you must have just missed it!"

"Just missed what?"

"The man who fell off the building. He fell from the Acheron Estate!"

"What man? Who jumped?" Eve questioned, setting her tea on the coffee table.

"The man fell from Acheron?" Finley questioned. He was now on his feet. His first thought told him it was Hansel. But surely it couldn't have been Hansel. While the man was no doubt an odd duck, he wasn't the sort to have jumped off a building.

Behind him, Eve kept asking Natalie and Finley who they were referring to, but each paid her no mind. Natalie kept rambling about how bizarre the occurrence was. Finley, meanwhile, was rummaging in his pockets for the business card that Hansel had first given him as he welcomed Finley into his office.

"Hush, girls. I've got to make an important phone call." There, standing in the hallway with the receiver firmly pressed against his left ear, he dialed the number.

The phone rang five times before it was picked up. "Hello?" A deep voice answered.

"Good afternoon, this is Mr. Finley Glover. I'm an acquaintance of Mr. Hansel Park. Is he available for a quick word?"

"No, Mr. Glover. I'm afraid Mr. Park can't come to the phone."

8

GONE LIKE A JACK RABBIT

The ringing in Hassle's head didn't hurt as much as the sound of the police officer's boots on the ground did. The thuds that accompanied the boots caused his head to feel as if it would split open. The constant vibration made him think he was going to become nauseated at any second. And the last thing this carpet needed was another stain.

"Can you turn down the volume?" Hassle snapped bitterly from the white gurney he lay on in Hansel's office. He gripped his left leg and winced.

The pressure from the tourniquet was helping to reduce the blood flow, but the wound painfully stung.

Officers closest to him attempted to oblige, but those farther down the hallway who couldn't hear his plea continued as normal.

"Sir, I've got you a cup of tea here and some tablets for your head."

Hassle mumbled a thanks before focusing his attention on the tea and the sour tablets that caused his lips to pucker. "Good God, Man. Have these expired?"

"No, sir. Dr. Shipley said that they've only recently been placed in the first aid kit."

"I doubt that very much. Dr. Shipley is a liar and a thief."

"He is also the one who searched high and low so that you can have an ice pack to treat that sizable bump on the back of your head. We've got to get you to the hospital," Dr. Shipley advised as he navigated through the crowd and delicately placed the ice pack against the bruised area.

Hassle shook his head, "You said yourself that it was just a flesh wound. I won't die."

"I said it wasn't a major hit. I never said it was minor and that a trip to the hospital wasn't needed," Shipley retorted.

Groaning, Hassle lay back down on the gurney and allowed Shipley to hold the pack in place.

When he came to some twenty minutes earlier, he realized almost at once that he was alone in the room. His mind initially tried to convince him that he should be alone. But his fingers told a different story. The hand that grasped the service weapon warned him that before he lost consciousness, he was on guard. He should, therefore, remain on guard.

With his firm grip on the gun and ready to raise at a second's notice, Hassle did his best to think about the events that transpired. He knew he squeezed the trigger. He saw the man opposite him fall to the ground with a dramatic thud. Hansel Park. Yes, it had been Hansel. But where was he now? Had he slumped behind the desk? Did Hassle make or miss his target? He needed to know.

Only when these thoughts penetrated his mind did he become more aware of his own situation. He was positioned awkwardly against the wall opposite the desk. His bum flat on the filthy carpet, while his legs were perfectly straight and still. Moving his neck to see around the desk, a fierce, sharp pain radiated, starting from the back of his neck down his spine. Shocked and afraid, Hassle slowly returned to his original position. Why was he feeling so sore? What had gone wrong?

"Steady on, lad," he whispered to himself as beads of sweat blinded his eyes. Sweat. The realization hit him almost immediately. Hansel had left another parting shot. He'd closed the only window that brought desperately needed comfort.

"Bollocks," he shouted into the empty office. The bastard had gotten away. He was gone—long gone—and Hassle was suffering in the hellhole Hansel created.

Screw it all, he thought, closing his eyes. Dying in the Thames didn't sound so bad now. He didn't know how long he'd been out before he felt a man's hand on his shoulder. Shaking it quickly and rather harshly, the man leaned forward and spoke loudly to Hassle.

"Sir, stay with me. I've got help coming behind me. We'll catch the bloke who did this. Can you hear me?"

"Good, God. You're four inches from my face. How can I not hear you? And the culprit's name is Hansel Park. English nationality," Hassle said flatly before launching into Hansel's descriptors: brown eyes, a nose that had been broken and never re-paired, medium height and weight, enjoyed a good cigar, and had a scar on the right jawline.

Hassle's eyes remained closed. Only after the irritation of Hansel fleeing from the room lessened did Hassle feel a slight burning feeling in his lower right calf. He didn't need to examine the wound to know it was just a grade above a flesh wound. While wondering how much he'd bled out, Man grabbed him from under his arms and raised him to his feet.

"Here we go," Man assessed as he continued to hold Hassle upright.

The sound of the gurney dinging a nearby corner brought Hassle some comfort. At least his suffering on the carpet ended. With his eyes cracked open, he took one more look at the carpet before noticing something in the corner of the room.

"Hold up," Hassle ordered.

Man obeyed. "Sir?"

"Look at that area rug next to the fake tree. Yes, that one. Pull it up."

Man obliged and carefully, with gloves now on, rolled up the carpet, revealing a sizable bloodstain. Even from a considerable distance, Hassle detected that the blood was recent. "Bloody hell," Man croaked.

"It's a bloody something, but I need to know if the blood belongs to Mr. Park. Check for a trail."

"There was no blood splatter or trail when we arrived," a constable to the far right of the room interjected.

"A trail. Look for a trail," Hassle snapped. "A trail from behind the desk to that area on the carpet. I shot at Hansel Park. There's a chance he collapsed there, but I'll only know for certain if I can see a trail going from A to B, so get to it."

"Aye." Using a pocket torch, Man did as ordered. First, he walked the short path. When nothing caught his eye, he crouched and carefully paced across the path. He was inches away from the blood stain when he'd drawn his conclusion. Propping his hand on the wall for support, he turned toward Hassle's direction. "No trail."

"Fine then," Hassle said, frustrated. Where had the blood come from? The blood was too far away from him for it to be his. Besides, not once during his conversation with Hansel had he been standing in that area.

"I suppose I'll report this to forensics. They can take photographs and maybe even a sample," Man speculated, as he pressed more firmly onto the wall to raise himself from the crouched position he'd maneuvered himself into.

While mid-air, his eyes shifted to the direction of the wall, and he stopped suddenly in his tracks. With his left hand pressed against the wall, he raised his right hand and gently knocked on the area close to his left hand. A soft thud sounded. Curious as to why the wall sounded odd, Man delivered a calculated punch to the wall. There was no mistaking it—both he and Hassle heard it. The sound was hollow.

"Kick it in," Hassle directed.

Without any hesitation, Man kicked the wall in. His boot went through the plaster and entered a vast space of emptiness.

"Some more kicks should do it," Man muttered.

After a series of hard kicks, Man stepped back and admired his handiwork. He, once again, crouched down and, with his trusted torch, shone a light into the hole. "Sir, I know you're unwell at the moment, but you're going to have to take a look at it."

Seconds after the last word left Man's mouth, a new flood of officers arrived on the scene. Several of them now held cameras and were eager to take as many pictures of the dingy office as possible. Another officer started canvassing the area to see what was worth bagging up as evidence. A brave man near the same age as Man had the audacity to start questioning Hassle about the struggle that occurred in the room.

Hassle shouted for silence. More than a few officers looked at one another, wondering what they were to do. The camera flashes slowly faded, and three officers left the room, just as Shipley entered with a new ice pack.

"Help me up, old boy," Hassle demanded.

Shipley obliged, "Here, you hold on to the gurney, and I'll hold onto the pack. There we go. Easy does it. Are you feeling any better? If I look hard enough, I might be able to scrounge up a strong dose of morphine."

Entranced by what lay before Man, Hassle shook his head and said somewhat dismissively, "Don't tempt me. I'll be right as rain in a few."

"Here, drink your tea. Fluids always do well for

the body."

"After this, Shipley," Hassle said, casting his eyes to where Man was positioning. "After this."

With wobbly feet, an ice pack pressed against the back of his head, and a leg that was becoming increasingly sore, Hassle joined Man in front of the hole. Inside, skeletal remains greeted him.

"Good God," Hassle muttered. "Move the light to the right. Move in if you have to—just don't touch the bones."

"Yes, sir."

Hassle gave Man a few moments to survey the area before asking, "Anything else?"

"There's company alright. I think I see the makings of another skeleton. There might be two."

"Right. Well, that still doesn't explain the blood stain. It's too fresh. Look, you've got some on your trouser leg. Not as nimble as you thought you were, huh? Give me a hand up, will you?"

"Should I call it in?" The number of forensics technicians on site was plenty to assist with Hassle's attack. Having more, however, would greatly assist in scoping out the entire floor, if not the entire building.

"Might as well. At the bare minimum, we've got several dead people holed up in a wall and the suspected murderer on the run. Put out an all-points bulletin."

"You think this Hansel Park is responsible?"

"I do. Before our altercation, he mentioned he'd been in this room for over twenty-seven years. Some sort of medical condition kept him a prisoner in here."

"What sort of medical condition? A phobia, is it?"

Hassle took a sip of tea, "That's what I theorized, but Hansel just laughed, and then he told me I disappointed him."

"You disappointed him?" Man repeated, skeptically.

"I wasn't enough," Hassle muttered. Internally, his mind was putting the broken pieces together. It might have been the tablets dispensed to him by Dr. Shipley, or it could be the adrenaline that surged throughout his body now that he was focusing on an investigation and not himself, but he was finally able to remember what Hansel had said to him.

Both guns went off. Both men fell to the ground. But once the shock wore off, only one man stood up.

Picking himself off the floor, Hansel gripped his left shoulder. A small stream of blood was slipping through his fingers.

"Just a graze, old boy," Hansel said nervously while applying more pressure to the area.

Hassle recalled his own mouth moving, but he didn't know what he'd said. Whatever he said caused Hansel's left eyebrow to rise and for him to shake his head in apparent disgust.

"I always thought detectives were men of intelligence, you know? They held an air of suaveness and sophistication," Hansel said, as he shakily made his way from behind his bulky desk. "I've read so many stories about police exploits, but then I met one, and I realized how bunk all of it was. You aren't impressive. You fell into my trap. They've all fallen into my trap. Yet, I think I'll be kind to you. I'll let you live. But you need to promise to catch me. If you don't, everything will have been for naught."

Staggering toward Hassle with a moronic grin resting on his face, Hansel continued to put pressure on his wound. When Hansel was close enough to Hassle, he leaned forward and tapped the pocket where Hassle placed his list of names, "Don't you forget. Important stuff. It's best I get a move on. We'll catch up when the time's right."

"Sir, can you hear me? Are you with me?" Man asked worriedly. His wide, blue eyes shifted around the room. Perhaps there was some sort of shot that Dr. Shipley could dispense.

Hassle focused back on the present. "I hear you. I was thinking back. We're on double time. We have a lunatic on the run. Listen, after you do what I've just told you, bring me another cuppa and one of those tablets. Then, see about getting me another ice pack. This one has run wet."

Man hopped to, leaving Hassle alone once more with his own thoughts. None of this made any sense. How had he fallen victim to such a ridiculously lunatic person? How had he not seen the metaphoric writing on the wall? Why hadn't he called for backup? He should have had Man or someone else trail him when he went to interview Hansel.

No, he thought. He couldn't let his doubts get the best of him. He hadn't made an error in judgment. He'd gone to collect a witness statement, not interview a potential suspect. He'd followed protocol.

"Has the phone been fingerprinted yet?" Hassle asked as he wobbled to the phone on Hansel's desk.

"Yes, sir. It was the first item we processed," a member of the forensic unit said. "Brittle's already shipped them off."

Hassle gave a sharp nod and dialed Scotland Yard's main line. Annie answered, "Scotland Yard."

"It's Hassle 5-8-9-9."

"Good afternoon, Hassle. Who can I transfer you to?" Annie asked in a slightly brighter tone than when she answered.

"Is Esther around? I need her assistance with a case I was just called on."

"I'm not sure. I haven't seen her about. Hold tight. I'll transfer you to her desk."

"Righty-o."

As Hassle waited for Esther to pick up, he leaned on the desk to take pressure off his right leg. From behind him, the forensic team was retrieving the skeletal remains from the hole in the wall. He glanced over to check their progress and took notice of how delicately and respectfully they were placing the bones in sealed-off bags.

He drummed his fingers on the edge of Hansel's desk. There was more to this blasted Hansel Park. It wasn't a phobia that kept him confined to a room in this hellhole of a building. No, it was something much more sinister. If only his bullet had gone just a little further right, he'd be in an interrogation room with Hansel. But he wasn't.

"Bastard," he seethed.

"It's always pleasant talking to you as well," a woman's voice with a slight Kingston accent said from the other end of the line.

"Sorry, Esther. It's not you, it's me. I've just realized the full scope of my predicament. I think it's high time I turn in the badge and take up golfing."

"Retirement would look good on you. No more stress or annoyance. You can simply drink tea and complain about the weather. Don't you English typically take up gardening? The Scots golf, no?"

Hassle sensed the smile on her face, and his mood immediately lifted. "I love where your mind goes."

"As does Scotland Yard, which explains why

I'm here. Now, why are you holding up my line?"

"You've received that certification in profiling?"

"I have it hanging proudly on the wall in front of my desk. You would know that if you ever took the time to visit me."

"I'm rubbish. I'll do better, I swear. Listen, I'm going to share some characteristics related to a person of interest. If I do that, do you think you can work up a profile?"

"What sort of person of interest? Murderer? Rapist?" Esther inquired.

He heard the sound of paper being shuffled around. If he had to guess, she was reaching for a notebook to jot down the information he was about to share with her.

"Murderer," Hassle answered bluntly before carrying on, "I suppose you've heard by now of the jumper from the Acheron Estate? The chap that I was interviewing has a space here in the building. His name is Hansel Park." He paused to spell the name out. "An altercation arose between him and me, which resulted in him fleeing. Only God knows what he's up to now."

"Did you say Acheron Estate?"

"I did."

"Why did you call it that?"

"That was the name given to me. What am I supposed to call it?"

"The Acheron Institute."

Looking around to make sure no one could hear what he was about to say, Hassle said softly, "Institute of what?"

"The criminally insane."

Hassle's gut dropped, "You can't be pulling my chain."

"I'm not, and I wouldn't when dealing with a murderer. I read about Acheron years ago when I was studying psychology at university. This must have been in '45."

"Are you saying that my officers are standing inside a mental institution?"

"Yes and no."

"Do go on," Hassle said sourly.

"Calm down and breathe. You're fine. You're an experienced and skilled detective who, by the sounds of it, is surrounded by other trained officers."

Then, without being prompted, Esther provided the limited information she knew about Acheron.

"The institute was built in 1835. It was created for and designed by the upper echelon of English society. Being wealthy does little to prevent mental issues like bipolar disorder and schizophrenia. They wanted a place where they could ensure their loved ones received the best care."

"I thought that lot shipped the odd duck to some back-wood village in some European country that no one goes to?"

Esther shrugged, "Maybe some, but not all."

"Did they not know what Acheron meant?" Hassle was far from being a scholar, but even he recognized the meaning behind the name.

"Who knows? I wasn't there when the concept was created. Perhaps someone thought putting a classic element in the building would give it an air of seriousness."

"I heard it was supposed to be residential flats for the rich."

"That's correct. Within the walls of Acheron, the committed lived a somewhat normal existence, minus the nurses and doctors who treated and monitored them."

"If the wealthy and elite created and funded this place, why does it look like absolute rubbish?"

Esther sighed, "They—the wealthy clients—began to lose trust in the establishment. All sorts of rumors began spilling out. Those paying for their loved ones to be committed and cared for believed that the owner of the institute was pocketing money by allowing journalists to sneak in to see who had been admitted. Almost overnight, patients were removed and placed into private, isolated institutes."

"But people are still occupying it. Why are they here?"

"Once the wealthy moved their loved ones out,

all sorts of investors became interested in the building. To be fair, it had potential. You should see the pictures of it when it was in its full glory. Each time an investor started to make serious progress, some sort of major hurdle occurred, making them lose interest," Esther paused to take a sip of water. "That was until Samual Acorn came along. He witnessed firsthand the devastating toll that depression and other forms of mental illness can have on a person. It's rumored his wife suffered from what we know as postpartum depression. During the depression, she suffered from some sort of fit that led to her smothering their newborn. Fueled by the loss, he purchased the property and eventually brought the building up to code. Gathering an impressive medical staff, he started to admit patients into the institution. By all accounts, he had good intentions, and the program was generally beneficial. Social reformers applauded his efforts to help the lower middle class."

"Then what?" he questioned.

At this point, Hassle looked behind him and saw that all the skeletal remains were out of the wall.

"After Acorn died, his nephew took over. I want to say this was in the late 1930's. But then the war and the blitz happened. Most of the building was blown to bits. The general assumption floated around that the building would be demolished."

"Weren't people concerned about the well-being of the patients? Where would they go if they were displaced?"

"I think mentally unfit people were the least of the government's worries," Esther said, now leaning closer to the phone.

"Who's running it now?"

"I'd have to look at public records. It could still be in the Acorn family, or it could still be vacant, and those in need are just squatting."

"No, patients are still here. I know it." It'd been too quiet. There were no open doors or feet shuffling about. The list Hansel provided also lent credence to Hassle's belief.

"Did you still want that profile?"

"I need a list of patients who were placed here. I have a feeling that Mr. Park was committed at the time Acorn's nephew took over. Speaking of whom, I need the nephew's name and contact information."

"If he's not alive?"

"Someone in the Acorn family must be aware of the mess that is Acheron."

The two hung up. Esther reviewed her to-do list, picked up the phone, and called a contact at the Charity Hospital. Hassle, meanwhile, surveyed the area around him. Like a coach shouting to his players on a pitch, he cupped his hands around his mouth, "All eyes and ears on me. Shout it down if you must—I want every officer in the building to be in this room. Now." He dragged out the word "now" until his throat became sore.

From the far-right corner of Hansel's main office, Shipley shook his head and pointed to Hassle's leg. Hassle, in turn, ignored the look and gesture. Instead, he focused on opening the windows closest to him. Some nails were securely in place. Others looked as if a good shake would open them up completely.

The sound of shuffling feet and men muttering to one another echoed throughout the room. Man was the tenth police officer to enter the room. He went straight to Hassle and delivered the tablet and the tea.

"Thank you," Hassle said, accepting the cuppa and gesturing for Man to stand next to him.

"Can you open that window there? That's the one. Try opening that one too. That one's nailed shut? Try using your pocketknife. Right then, now go try that one. That's a good chap."

By now, all the windows in the room were allowing a much-needed breeze to wash over the officers. A fresh rain smell filled the room, alerting Hassle that a light afternoon shower had accompanied him as he lay unconscious on the floor.

"First and foremost, I want to thank the forensic team that processed the scene as quickly and effectively as they did." With that acknowledgment being issued, Hassle started a round of applause. A few members of the forensic team raised an arm to accept the praise. "Also, Dr. Shipley. Thank you for staying with us instead of returning to the Yard. I, for one, am grateful for your presence."

Another round of applause.

"Right then, onto business as it were. Everything you might have heard about this building is wrong. At the start of the investigation, this building was nothing more than a series of office spaces." A few officers nodded their heads. "That is a bald-faced lie. This *estate* is actually a former mental institution that we will be searching from top to bottom." A few officers tensed up and looked at their colleagues. "I know that's not something you want to hear, but I want you to know that firstly, you're trained and skilled officers of the law. Secondly, I believe this building is empty. The last two residents are no more. One was murdered this morning, and the other is on the lam. Thirdly, you will be working in pairs. We have our work cut out for us. Murder on more than one occasion has occurred in this building. Our own officer, Man, found what looks to be the skeletal remains of two people."

This time, there was no round of applause, but several officers bobbed their heads.

"Once I release you from this huddle, we will tear this building apart from top to bottom. Every wall will be knocked down. Every bit of carpet will be removed. Every room will be inspected. You—we—will not go home until every last square inch has been searched and analyzed. Go make phone calls to your wives or girlfriends and let them know your hot date is on hold. Off you go, then. Man, start leading the officers. Go to the ground floor and work your way up. I expect all of you to know the proper procedures for group searches. If you don't, I don't want to know or hear about it. Follow what your fellow experienced officers are doing."

"Sir, is there anyone or anything in particular we're looking for?" Man tentatively asked.

From his breast pocket, Hassle handed Man the list Hansel provided him hours earlier, "Careful, not to lose that. In fact, why don't you make a copy before you head off?"

Man did as directed. With multiple copies, Man and his fellow officers uniformly departed with concentrated looks. Hassle felt a sense of pride.

Before he could turn his attention to Shipley, who was waiting to insist that Hassle go to the hospital to avoid infection, the phone on Hansel's desk rang.

9

More Tea for Me

Martha bent over and rubbed her ankles with her fingertips. It wasn't her age, she assured herself. It was the heat.

Pulling up her stockings, she shuffled to the front door and flipped the sign so that the "closed" side was facing out onto the street. It'd been a long day. First with the jumper and then with the detective questioning her. There was more to be done, yet the thought of a nice, long soak in the tub flashed in her mind. She might even reward herself with a glass of white wine. Red always gave her a headache.

"Eric, I'm going to the back to work on payroll. When you've done cleaning up, go on home. I'll see you bright and early tomorrow."

Eric turned from pouring the dirty floor water down the sink and stared at her with a blank expression. "I have tomorrow and the next day off, ma'am. You'll next see me on Friday. It'll be bright and early then."

"Well, yes. Alright, then. Go on with your duties."

Nodding, Eric collected the cotton rags and spray bottle filled with the cleaning detergent needed to wipe off the tabletops and counters. Martha gave him one last look before shaking her head. *Such a simpleton*, she thought. *Is it a curse or a gift?*

Setting herself down in the normally awkward steel chair, she closed her eyes and exhaled a breath of air. How nice it felt! How could Eric, Natalie, and Brandon be on their feet all day and still waltz out of the shop at closing time light on their feet?

Maybe it was time she did something nice for them. She could give them a voucher to their favorite shop or maybe a raise. Seeing as how Natalie was a university student and the two young lads were always attempting to pick up the cute birds that walked in, she figured a raise might be the better option.

From the pouch she carried from the front of the shop, she pulled out receipts and cash from the tills. She hadn't counted them yet, but given her time and experience on the job, she'd be correct in guessing they exceeded their average.

At first, she thought the jumper might have dampened business for the shop, but the opposite had happened. Once the police put up the barrier that prevented onlookers from seeing the bodies, they removed the blockade. Now, those who wanted the skinny on what happened used her tea shop as an excuse to be in the area. No matter how busy they got, Martha never failed to doubt her decision to let Natalie and Brandon go.

Natalie, what a smart but delicate girl. Such a diligent employee. Martha was both stunned and impressed when Natalie shared that she was majoring in economics. What a masculine topic. Martha didn't feel embarrassed by her profession, but she did briefly wonder if Natalie thought less of her. Dispensing tea for a living was hardly impressive.

Why did what Natalie thought matter? Well, Martha supposed it didn't. Martha wouldn't like to admit it, but she held a special interest in young women. Not in a romantic way, just in an interested way, as if she were curious about them. She knew what her curiosity stemmed from, even if she dared not say it out loud. Not even Tom knew of her little secret. It wasn't a little secret—not really. It was a secret that was best kept in her heart.

Pencil in hand, Martha began tallying figures of the day when the back door burst open. Frozen in fear, Martha sat perfectly still, not to give away her presence. It did her no good, as the person who'd burst through the door did so for a private word with her.

"Martha," Tom gasped out of breath. He clutched the doorway for support.

"Tom, what are you doing here? I wasn't expecting you for a few more hours."

As Martha was typically Tom's last stop, he usually dropped by around six. After the shop closed, she'd stay in the back working on the finances. Once that was done, she'd get herself something to eat. She'd typically opt for fish and chips or a meat pie. To further pass the time, she'd sometimes read a book.

"What's going on? You mentioned a jumper."

"Here, drink this water. Why are you so worked up about a jumper?" Martha laughed softly, in hopes that it would break up the tension within the room. It did not.

"Tell me about the man who jumped."

"I know nothing about the man who jumped. I mean, I don't think I do. I didn't get a look at his face."

"Did the police come around?" When Martha didn't answer immediately, he practically shouted,

"Tell me! Did the police come around? Were they questioning people? Did they question you?"

"Get a hold of yourself, Tom. Yes, I was questioned. It was standard protocol."

Tom rubbed his hands together. "You gave your name?"

Martha nodded.

"Good, of course you did," Tom said. "What else would you have done? Given them someone else's name. Very well. You did good. Now tell me, did you give them my name?"

Martha looked on in fright as Tom roughly licked his lips. "Why would I give them your name?"

"Did they ask about me?"

"Why would they ask about you, Tom? Do you do deliveries there? You've never said as much before."

"Stop asking me questions and just answer mine," he shouted so fiercely at her that specs of spit sprayed on her chin.

"If you don't calm down and get a grip on yourself, I'm going to have to ask you to leave," Martha snapped. She was not the type of person who did well with being yelled at. Her worry for Tom kept her in check, but the testier he became, the more her attitude changed.

Rubbing his bald head and pacing back and forth, Tom laughed, "You think I'm a problem? Oh, love, you know nothing about problems. The real problem is all around us." He stopped laughing and covered his eyes with his rough hands. "This is so bad. It's beyond bad. I had one job. One job, and it went tits up. He's going to have my arse."

"You need to calm down. This isn't about you. You did nothing wrong."

Tom dropped his hands, "You know how you always go on about the people across the street being odd? I've got news to tell you, love. They're worse than odd. Far worse. You couldn't even imagine the likes of those people."

"Here, there's some tea that hasn't been poured out. I'll pour you a cup. You've had a stressful day. I know you, Tom. You just need to breathe in and out." The kindness and concern in her voice did little to calm Tom's nerves.

"I got out," Tom pounded on his chest, a look of pride evident in his eyes. "I did what they asked. I did well, and they let me out. They let me walk out the doors, but there was a catch. There's always a catch. If I didn't make myself available to them, they said they'd take me back in. They had the connections to do so. I knew they weren't playing around."

Martha moaned and returned to her seat.

"Once I got my posting, I'd drop things off here and there when I could. They liked that. They said I was doing a good enough job. But I was also supposed to be keeping my eye on the lot that stayed there. They told me who could leave and who had to stay."

Her blood ran cold at seeing the man whom she had once loved so unconditionally in such a disturbed state. Feeling faint, she feared that at any moment she might slip onto the ground. She wanted Tom to stop. She didn't want or deserve an explanation.

"When he hears about this, I'm as good as gone. I'll be in the Thames."

"Slow down a minute."

"I can't let them find me. The game's up, Martha. I can't show my face anymore. If I do," Tom shook his head but didn't finish his thoughts.

"Here, take this," Martha hurriedly scooped up a handful of pounds from the two tills. "Take this and go. They can't hurt you if they can't find you." As she didn't know who 'they' were, she didn't know how truthful her statement was, but at least she was making an effort.

Tom looked at the money being presented to him. He slowly stepped back from her.

Marth stepped forward, "Go on, take it. Take it and go. Who has to know?"

"You mean it?" Tom asked dubiously. "I can have this? I don't know if I'll ever be able to repay you."

"I needn't be repaid. I'll be fine. Go to wherever

you feel safe. If anyone asks, I'll tell them I don't know anything about you. Please, go now. There are more police coming by in a minute. If you need to run, go."

Tom leaped forward as if to kiss her, but he hugged her instead. With his chest pressed firmly against hers, he whispered into her ear, "I was always a good boy. They told lies to get me committed. You ask all who knew me back then, they'd tell you I was a good lad. I always did good and acted right. My mum's new husband didn't want me around. I was a reminder of my dad. There couldn't be two men in the house. You know me."

Frozen by a grip of panic, Martha kissed him on the cheek. "You're a good man, even if you're a dirty rascal."

"Knowing you has been the best part of my life."

He hugged her one more time before running out of the tea shop. Sitting down, Martha realized she was drenched in his sweat. Caught up in the panic his emotions provoked, she hadn't asked questions. Now alone in the kitchen, she refused to allow her mind to speculate. Still, the quickness of the escapade and his choice of words surprised her.

Committed? How could he have been committed to a building complex? He'd told her it was a complex of sorts. One of his mates confirmed it. He'd told her a few weeks after having first delivered a massive supply of tea and accessories. He was the one who told her about the blitz attack. It was he who fed her the lies about the building so that she was none the wiser.

She gasped and then instinctively covered her mouth with her hand. All this while, he'd made her feel horrible for calling the people who occupied the building horrible people, but if they were committed, they weren't horrible. Special? Needy? What was the term?

"No," she muttered to herself. She didn't want to know. She didn't want to know about the people he was referring to. She didn't need to know about the people who he thought were after him. She didn't want to know about the people he was supposed to look after.

With her nerves wrecked, she placed the tills in the safe located next to the makeshift desk. She'd deal with that mess either tonight or early tomorrow morning. After placing the key in its secret location, she reached for her handbag. More than anything, she needed the thick bound of freshly typed papers inside. It was a manuscript from an unpublished author.

Months earlier, Natalie realized she'd forgotten her jumper at the shop and had stopped by to collect it. Knocking on the back-alley doorway, Martha let her in. After profusely apologizing, Natalie grabbed her jumper, but not before noticing the book on Martha's desk. From there, the always chatty Natalie started talking about a recent mystery she'd just read.

Out of politeness, Martha nodded and listened to Natalie describe the murderer and the plot. Once that source of conversation dried up, Natalie switched topics to her best friend's father, Mr. Finley Glover. Martha's heartbeat accelerated, and the palms of her hands started to sweat. She felt grateful that Natalie couldn't tell.

"Oh, Mr. Glover is a tremendous writer. Eve is always giving me copies of his manuscripts. He's not published at the present, mind you, but he will be."

Martha, whose throat turned unexpectedly dry, attempted to take part in the conversation. "What does he write about?"

"Mostly about the Wild West. That's in the States. They're real capers, I can tell you that. That's how I learned about Billy the Kid, and wait, there's a woman who was known for being a sharpshooter."

"Calamity Jane," Martha answered, not missing a beat.

"Yes," Natalie said, snapping her fingers. "Then, there's this guy named Bill."

"Buffalo Bill."

"Do you like the Wild West?"

How could she not? That's all he talked about

when he was courting her. "I do. I like cowboys and lost gold mines very much."

"Next time I go back home, I'll ask Eve for a copy of the manuscript. I won't tell her what it's for. It can be our little secret. I mean, if you think about it, Mr. Glover is going to want to build a fan base, right?"

"Right. Wait, Natalie. Don't go. This friend of yours—Eve—is she a nice, clean girl? Is she studying at university?"

"Oh, Eve's a saint! She's incredibly sweet and kind. She's a bit on the shy side, but there's nothing wrong with that. I think she wants to study art, but funds are sort of tight. She only has her dad around. Her mum got sick a long time ago. She needs continuous treatment."

She was sick, not dead. That was a relief.

"Can you tell me more about your friend? You hardly ever mention anyone other than your classmates."

For the next ten minutes, Natalie regaled Martha about her and Eve's adventures. How they were Girl Scouts, how they got chicken pox at the same time, and how Eve had used her artistic abilities to help decorate Natalie's studio flat. By the time Natalie said her last goodbye, Martha felt proud and oddly justified. Maybe she hadn't made the wrong decision after all.

At present, Finley's book would serve as a

proper distraction. "Right then. Fin, let's have a look at chapter four, shall we?"

Within seconds, she was lost in the world of 1849 San Fransico. A madam at a brothel was shouting after a client who had roughed up a girl of hers. Threatening and using every swear word imaginable, the madam condemned the man to death. Nearby, a man new to gold prospecting overheard. Disgusted by both the woman's profession and the customer's cavalier way of laughing when he admitted to the atrocities he committed against the woman, the man new to town reached for his sharpshooter. Just as he was about to take aim, Martha received a real surprise—a hand placed light on her back.

"Sorry, Ms. Martha. Didn't mean to scare you. I wanted to make sure you knew I was leaving. I heard you a while back having a heated conversation. I didn't want to butt in, but now that I know you're safe, I figured it was okay."

"You're alright. I was reading and didn't hear you come in. Yes, a friend and I were having a passionate discussion, but I'm fine. Thank you for your work today. I'll see you later this week."

Although dismissed, Eric didn't leave out the back. Instead, he looked down at the manuscript in front of her. "Are you a writer, Ms. Martha?"

"Oh, no," Martha laughed furtively. She easily called Tom a friend, but Fin? What was Fin to her after all these years? "Someone else wrote this. Someone I know rather well."

"You don't have to be embarrassed. Anyone can be an artist. Take me, for instance. I'm a drummer. My band has a chance, you know? All sorts of people come to watch us perform. We've sold out a few pubs."

"You're a musician? That's wonderful. I'm glad so many people enjoy your music." Martha peppered Eric with questions about his music and the other band members, but his eyes focused on the manuscript.

"What's the book about? Anything to do with spies?"

"Not at the present. The book is about the Wild West."

"When did England have a Wild West?"

"The States, dear. You know, California, Arizona, and the like."

"I've heard of California. You know, my dad is a literary agent over at Chapel Press. He's always looking out for the next big writer. If you wanted me to, I could pass it over to him."

Now thoroughly flushed, as if her hand had been caught in the cookie jar, Martha cleared her throat, "It's not my book. Honest. It's somebody I know. He likes to write. He's been writing for years."

"Not the bloke who was shouting at you?"

"Oh, no. Definitely not the bloke who was shouting at me. No, it's an older friend. One I've known for longer who is incredibly sweet."

"I mean, it's whatever. If Dad likes the book, it doesn't matter who wrote it. What's your friend's contact information?"

She mulled it over for a brief moment before declaring, "His name is Finley Glover. I'll write down his home address."

10

<u>Goodbyes Never Last</u>

He hadn't planned on arriving so late. The night sky was in full effect with only the stars and a handful of streetlamps to illuminate his way. While his current location was where he'd known he wanted to go, he didn't make it his first destination.

No, upon leaving Acheron, the first place he ventured to was a nearby pharmacy. The injury he'd sustained was minor, but it needed to be bandaged. While the cashier rang up his purchases, she occasionally glanced at the blood-soaked area but didn't ask any questions or make any small talk to gather information from him.

After tending to the wound, the real fun began. His second stop was the fish and chip shop that he'd seen through his bedroom window. The baskets were so big! Sometimes, without being asked, Tom would be a nice chap and deliver him a basket of fish and chips. But by the time the food reached him, it was always cold and soggy.

He'd received a few odd glances, but what did they expect? He was standing in line! He was out in public. Cars that he saw passing on the street were now at arm's length from him. He touched a tree. He'd even bought himself an ice lolly. He was now part of the outside world.

While Detective Chief Inspector Louis Hassle was a letdown, it gave him the final push he needed to leave his captivity. Little did Hassle know that he assisted Hansel in telling his story. Hansel briefly wondered how Hassle would answer the journalist's questions, for Hansel knew he didn't kill Hassle because he wasn't aiming to kill. No, he just needed to hurt Hassle to prove a point. He also needed someone to help spread his reputation. Some coppers liked doing that. They enjoyed nothing more than rehashing their most famous cases.

Tom wouldn't be happy. Tom would be scared. Hansel's confinement guaranteed Tom's freedom. But Hansel didn't hold that against Tom. No,

Hansel understood. At the end of the day, it was a dog-eat-dog world where someone suffered. Hansel was just tired of it being him.

Even in the dark, the terrace house where Finley and his daughter lived appeared charming and welcoming. Light shone through the off-white lace living room curtains. From a considerable distance, Hansel saw Finley and a young woman, probably in her late teens, laughing, at a television screen. What were the odds that if he knocked and was let in, he too would join them in the entertainment?

The news had yet to plaster his face on every television screen in the country. Therefore, he had the opportunity to cross a few more items off his bucket list. He might even return to the city. He'd yet to visit the Tower of London. His mum had been a huge fan of the attraction. She'd repeatedly threaten to lock him and his brother in the tower wall just like the two princes.

Yes, walls. His brother was in a wall. His brother, Magnus.

Magnus was the favorite twin, but Hansel was the special twin. It only took them all too long to figure out how truly special he really was. By the time they did, five worthless people were dead.

"Why did you do this? You're a bloody monster." Magnus said bleakly while trying to suppress the sickness forming in the back of his mouth.

He and Hansel were standing in an abandoned

football pitch that was overgrown with weeds and other forms of vegetation. Trash and various discarded materials were scattered throughout the area. Magnus didn't care much for the place because the less-than-desirable people who lived nearby frequented it. More than once, he'd told Hansel to steer clear of the place. But Hansel didn't listen. He never listened. That was his real problem.

"You don't even know her. Why do you care?"

"You slashed this poor bird's neck. What'd she do?"

The disbelief in Magnus's voice was earnest. Up to that point in his life, he'd never even raised his voice at a woman. Yet, here was his brother standing nonchalantly in front of a poor girl whose life he'd clearly taken. The joy in Hansel's eyes was sickening. Mangus turned away and looked at the sixteen-year-old deceased girl who lay on her back. Her brown eyes were open to the sky. A blood trail started at her neck and dripped down her shoulders. Aside from a cat that'd been skinned by some low-lifes that lived in the estate, Magnus had never seen something so awful in person.

"Nothing. I was bored," Hansel waved his hand that once held the knife used to murder her. "I was making my way home through that trail there. She smiled at me, and I saw that she was missing a tooth. I nodded to be polite. Manners, you know? For some ungodly reason, that small gesture gave her the impression that I wanted her to approach me. The nerve! As she grew closer, I saw the faint stains on her dress and the dirt under her fingernails. Trash. Pure, horrid trash. Give it a few more weeks, and she'd probably be working the streets. I thought I'd do society a favor, so I did away with her."

Magnus looked incredulously at his brother. His mind refused to accept that he'd made that rash, horrid split-second decision because his standards deemed her not worthy of life. "Tell me there was another reason."

"What good could she do to society? Look at her! Even in death, you can sense the stupidity that once radiated from her. She's some nitwit. Come off it. Look, I'll place her with the others. You won't have to think twice about it."

Magnus rubbed his forehead and groaned, "The others. There shouldn't be others."

"Listen, you're making a scene. If you can't handle the situation, perhaps you should be on your way."

"This isn't funny. You killed a person. You've killed people. Knock that smirk off your face."

"And if I don't?"

Without so much as a second thought, Magnus cocked back his right fist and aimed it at the center of Hansel's face. Shocked not by the pain, which had caused him to stumble backward, but by

Magnus's action, Hansel stuttered, "You punched me."

"Square up, brother, because I'll do it again."

"You wouldn't."

Hansel found out that Magnus would—because he did.

"What are you doing?" Hansel asked, pinching his nose to stop the bleeding. "Are you trying to avenge the deceased?"

"I'm trying to make you feel some sort of punishment for what you've done."

"Why would I be punished? Seriously, you're becoming such a bore. I would expect my brother—twin brother, at that—to be a little more understanding."

"Where are the others?"

"Obviously, in places where they won't be found."

Magnus landed another punch. This one knocked Hansel to the ground. While he lay in a fetal position, Hansel felt himself falling in and out of consciousness.

Leaning over him, Magnus said softly, "If you tell me where the others are, I can go about this the nice way."

Hansel's first thought was to say, "I don't like nice things," but the words that came out of his mouth were, "I'm afraid I've forgotten."

Straightening up, Magnus looked around them.

Determining that the coast was clear, he kicked Hansel's stomach with tremendous force. A stream of blood shot from Hansel's throat. "The hard way it is."

Days later, Hansel woke up in what would later become the office of his literary agency. He assessed the situation and made it a point to leave, but the front door was locked. He went to the windows and tried to open them. They were nailed shut. With as much force as he could muster, he realized not a single window would budge. Moving away from the windows, he started to pound on a connecting wall.

"Can anyone hear me?" Hansel shouted at the wall.

"You can make as much noise as you want," Magnus replied. "Your cries fall on deaf ears."

Before submitting his brother, Magnus asked thorough and detailed questions as to how secure his brother would be. Security, the overseer of the institute said, was as tight as a prison. As of yet, there had yet to be an escapee, and as long as he worked at the institute, there wouldn't be one. Orderlies were dutifully assigned not only to monitor attendants but also to stand guard in locations that prevented escape. Hearing what he needed to hear, Magnus signed the papers.

Hansel slowly turned around and locked eyes with Magnus, who was standing in the hallway that led to the front door. Pushing aside the thought of how long Magnus had been present in the flat, Hansel asked. "Where am I?"

"Acheron."

"No. No. There's no way," Hansel muttered in horror while frantically shaking his head. "You wouldn't do that to me."

Magnus couldn't be serious. He'd heard of Acheron. Who hadn't? It was a common taunt within the council estate that he lived in with his family: if naughty children didn't behave, they'd be locked away in Acheron. That's where the naughty people went. Of course, the children knew there was truth hidden in the adult's taunts.

There'd been a few people from their row who had been dragged from their homes by intimidating figures dressed in all-black suits. The individuals loading the panicked people weren't coppers nor were they council workers. They were a class all to their own. A group of people all within the estate learned to fear. In terror, the people being forcefully removed from their homes shrieked that they were fine people and that they were sorry for their transgressions. They would be better. It was an accident. They pleaded until their voices went hoarse—that they didn't want to go.

Only after the distressed people were loaded into the back of the wagon and the black-suited people were long gone, did the remaining residents quietly gather. Murmurs of what the taken person did ran rampant among them. One such person who was snatched in the middle of the night was James Preston. Rumor had it that he'd been improper with some children in the park. That he'd tried to lure the children into a wooded area nearby. Others said that because James made his living selling sweet rolls, he was simply trying to get the children to come to his cart. Whatever the reason, James was never seen again.

While they might not know the cause of his departure, they knew his destination. Acheron's reputation was legendary. It was rumored that once the intended patients vacated the premises, doctors and nurses started to collect people off the street so that they could perform ghastly experiments.

"You didn't give me much of a choice, did you? Besides, I've been called up to service. I'm off to fight in France. The last thing I need is my murderous brother on the prowl, making life more difficult for people who have it rough already."

"Why not send me to jail? Wouldn't you like that? Wouldn't you like to see me paraded through the street like some wild animal?" Hansel sneered.

"There'd be nothing better than to see you at the end of a short rope, but unfortunately, I don't think Mum would be able to bear it. So, I think this place will do instead. Oh, and don't worry about Mum. To her, you're dead. It's better that way."

"How did I die?"

"You drowned while fishing. I tried to save you, but you were too far upstream for me to grab you."

Nervously, Hansel drummed his fingertips on the desk in front of him. "I'll tell you where the others are."

"Too late. Once I knocked you out, I anonymously phoned the police. I told them about the dead girl and how there might be others. They've since found them." Magnus explained, looking at Hansel as if he were the devil. The few details released in the newspapers about the five murders were absolutely disgusting. Balling up one newspaper and throwing it in the bin, Magnus wondered how his own twin brother could commit such atrocities.

"Have they given me a nickname? You know how the press is. Am I a ripper of sorts?"

"Thank you for saying what you just said. I now know for sure you're in the correct place. If I get back, we can reassess your situation."

"What if you don't?"

"You'll regret the day you ever murdered those innocent little swans."

"Oh, you know nothing about those pieces of filth."

"Maybe not. But I know murder is wrong." Magnus stood from the mustard-colored settee. "You'll be under lock and key. Don't even think about escaping."

"What shall I do to pass the time?"

"A bookstore was going out of business, so I picked up some. You like to read, right? So, there you go. A little something to pass the time." To the left of Magnus and the settee were five modestly sized brown boxes crammed full of books. Some leather-bound; others paperback. All were more than he deserved.

"So, after you beat me an inch close to death, you decided to place me in some damnable mental institution? Then, in a random act of kindness, you purchased me reading material? Such a good brother you are." Hansel said with a smirk. But in a split second, his smirk shifted to a frown, and he slammed his fist against the wall, yelling, "You have no right to lock me up!"

"You had no right to murder," Magnus retorted menacingly.

"What if I'm called to fight? I'd have to respond. I'd hate to be considered a deserter." Hansel taunted.

Magnus answered by slamming the door closed as he departed the room.

Filled with feelings of anger, betrayal, and con-fusion, Hansel ignored the books given to him by Magnus. Only out of necessity did he eat the food delivered by an orderly wearing a face mask meant to disguise their identity. From the build of the person, he figured the person to be a man. A man much bigger than Hansel.

In the months that followed, Hansel's resolve started to fade. He stopped pacing between the rooms and eyed the books in the brown boxes. After being threatened with a lobotomy by a gruff orderly, he stopped banging on the windows. He was too high up. No one looked up. No one noticed him.

Years later, when the Luftwaffe bombs caused heavy destruction to the building, Hansel naively thought he saw a way out. But it was not to be. Under the darkness of night, the orderlies and supervisors got to work. Cleaning up most of the debris themselves, they hired a repair crew to rebuild the side of the wall, exposing the vacant walls. The inhabitants killed by the bomb blast were all but forgotten about.

Years later, Magnus did return, and the two did reassess the situation. Scared of horrors that kept him up at night, Magnus decided not to let Hansel go. Not yet. No, he would continue to pay the fee that kept Hansel contained.

"It's time you made something of yourself. You can't spend all day doing nothing," Magnus said while taking in the room around him. While he didn't know outright what Hansel could do to rehabilitate himself, he couldn't let Hansel pass his time by reading books and living off his dime.

Hansel reluctantly had made a home for himself. The books Magnus purchased for him lined the walls in black built-in bookshelves. Clearly, Hansel had made a friend.

"I've been thinking the same thing, actually."

"Is that so?" Hansel remarked, not trying to hide his surprise.

"Yes. You see, the books you've given me have inspired me to make a career choice perfect for someone with my skill set."

"Which is?" Magnus didn't know Hansel had any skill sets aside from murdering innocent women.

Hansel paused and looked at his brother's sunken eyes. If the war didn't consume him, the flashbacks would. "A literary agent."

"Out of the question," Mangus replied instantaneously.

"What? Why not?" Hansel asked, genuinely shocked.

"To be a literary agent, you've got to meet with people. We can't have people entering and exiting the establishment." Hansel sniggered at the word *establishment.* "If people get the likes of you, they'd surely leave petrified by your presence."

Hansel ignored the insult and continued with his planned argument, "False. On all accounts. First, the policies have changed, depending on the patient's diagnosis. No, don't interrupt me. I didn't interrupt you. People are coming and going all the time. Surely, you saw Sally in the hallway. You didn't think she worked here, did you? I hear her ramblings all day long. She hears voices, but they say nice things; therefore, she's not a threat."

He desperately wanted to say more about those who lived within Acheron Estate. The real horror of his confinement was missing the joys of everyday living. Going to the cinema or a football match were things of the past. As was enjoying the company of women who'd gladly pleasure those who could afford it. The only company now was those who roamed the hallways. Unlike him, they were pathetic, destitute people with not an ounce of intelligence.

Throughout the years, they'd bang on his door, asking to come in and have a chat. At first, he'd rejected a good many of them. The last thing he needed was those sorts of people in his flat, touching his stuff while attempting to sound smart and stately. No, what a good many of them needed were straitjackets and pills that kept them in a medically induced coma. As the years progressed, Hansel became more open to the idea of letting someone venture into his flat. Magnus didn't need to know that.

"You are."

"Only to women—some women. Sally is still alive. I'm doing better. I've made progress. Isn't that the goal of these sorts of institutions? Besides, how many female writers do you know about?" Magnus promptly gave the names of eight female authors, all relatively well-known. "Enough, I get the point. I'll compromise. I'll only ever invite male authors back here. Who knows? Perhaps with the money I generate, I can pay an orderly to stand and observe me from the other room. They do it already. Might as well chuck them a few bits and bobs to brighten their day."

"You'll need contacts within the publishing community."

"The pen is mightier than the sword, brother. If they want me to venture out to meet them, I'll come up with some sort of excuse. Aren't there people allergic to the sun? I can be a vampire."

Magnus wasn't yet convinced, but Hansel successfully planted a worm in his ear. He'd found work as a head gardener for the Cartwrights, an old, rich, stuffy couple, whose large manor employed ten other servants. But his back sustained considerable damage during the war. He didn't know how much he could keep working. Another source of revenue would help to alleviate the stress he felt.

Days later, Magnus returned to Hansel. "Make no mistake about it," he said, pointing a gnarled finger at Hansel, "if this venture goes awry, and you start acting out, I will rein you in. It'll be worse than it was before. I swear to you."

Hansel nodded. The giddy sensation he felt from the prospect of interacting with normal people who didn't suffer from mental abnormalities and being proactive again simmered under the surface.

Gradually, the capital was gathered for Ainsworth Press to begin. The small profit Ainsworth Press earned went into a bank account that secured him being confined in Acheron. True to his word, not once did Hansel murder a writer whom he hoped to sign on to Ainsworth Press.

Now, those who willingly ventured in because they thought the door was open or asked to come in-that wasn't his fault. Unfortunately, killing a man did not bring him the same thrill as killing a woman. But a thrill was a thrill, and beggars can't be choosers.

The only obstacle was knowing where to hide the bodies. After five years of him becoming a literary agent, the orderlies stopped coming around. The place was becoming a ghost town due to a lack of necessary funds. Now, in an odd turn of events, those suffering from mental illness willingly locked themselves within the building. It promised more security than the outside world. The inside allowed him the opportunity to pursue the two things he loved: literature and murder. As long as he was good with the former, he could get away with the latter.

His surroundings also became a solution: He'd hide the bodies in the wall. There weren't many bodies, and the walls were somewhat plentiful. Through Tom, who was none the wiser, he could get drywall and plaster. Only once had Tom ever questioned why Hansel needed the supplies. He claimed, falsely of course, that a bookshelf had fallen and, in the process, scraped a wall. It was enough for Tom.

He placed his brother's dead body in a wall whose hole had been prepared months earlier. Magnus wasn't faring well health-wise. It was cancer. He didn't confirm or deny the condition. He simply told Hansel to mind his business. But how could he? Magnus's business was Hansel's business. As far as Hansel knew, Magnus wasn't married. If Magnus died, no one would know of his confinement.

Magnus's condition and his conversation with Finley were the turning points that Hansel needed. For the fact of the matter, in his twenty-odd years as a literary agent, only six authors had ventured into his flat. Shortly thereafter, they'd turned down his offer of representation. The authors who agreed to be represented by Ainsworth Press had never met Hansel face to face. Oh, how he was grateful for the telephone. Finley Glover was the only person who'd met him and hadn't been repulsed by Hansel's personality and Acheron's dismal state.

The fact that Acheron was an institute for the mentally unfit was a secret kept only known by those who needed to know.

So, here he was taking Finley up on his offer. He probably hadn't expected Hansel to visit so soon. But Hansel knew that Finley was a good person. He wouldn't mind.

Well, Hansel thought to himself as he turned off the ignition and removed the key. *I shouldn't dawdle. If I do, I might miss the comedy on the telly. Yes, I would like to have a laugh with Finley and his daughter.* Hansel fantasized that upon seeing him, Finley would clasp him firmly on the shoulder and welcome him into the house. Hansel would treat the daughter fairly. Yes, no harm would come her way.

Standing on the pavement directly in front of their living room window, Hansel breathed the word home. He was home. Twenty years of solitude brought him home. He'd deserved this moment.

Also deserving of a moment was the person lurking in the shadows near the garage. He was the reason why the porch light was off. He was the reason that the lamps on the street directly in front of the rowhouse were turned off. But Hansel was the reason why six unmarked police cars were lined up in front of the houses nearby. It was Hansel who caused the man to aim his gun in Hansel's direction.

A light flickered in a nearby house. It was Man's signal that Hassle had the clear. Yet, Hassle wasn't the sort of man to shoot another man with his back to him.

Seeing Hansel's hands free of any weapon and at a reasonable location so that he couldn't easily withdraw a weapon, Hassle spoke slowly and clearly: "Funny seeing you here."

About the Author

Heather M Lewis was born in Illinois and raised in South Carolina. Her childhood consisted of reading books and daydreaming. After earning degrees in History and Library Information Science and having worked numerous positions from Shipping Technologist to Quality Specialist, she decided to pursue her passion for writing. In her free time, she still enjoys reading and day-dreaming, but she also takes pleasure in her old-lady hobbies, such as cross stitch and baking.